Beneath the Dune

A Novel by
WALTER RAMSAY

Pena Beach Press
New Jersey Florida

This is a work of fiction. Names, characters, places, and incidents
are products of the author's imagination or are used fictitiously.
Any similarity to actual events or locales or persons, living or
dead, is entirely coincidental.

For information about the author and future books:
www.walterramsay.com
penabeachpress@gmail.com

ISBN: 0983440700
ISBN-13: 9780983440703
Library of Congress Control Number: 2011924887

Printed in the United States of America

FOR MY CHILDREN:
RYAN, KERI, PATRICK,
&
NICKOLAS

Beneath the Dune

CHAPTER

1

Osci paddled his canoe with a sense of urgency. As thunder cracked and lightning strikes filled the sky, he glided along the shoreline, praying to go unnoticed in the darkness. Electricity radiated through the air as a storm blew in from the coast. Rain had not reached its fingertips to the little canoe. Thick moisture pervaded the air, engulfing Osci as he paddled along. In the dark of night, the flashes of lightning were the only thing that broke through the sky under its low cover of clouds. Their bright spears sparked across the water, leading his way, and Osci knew this was the only chance he had to escape and complete his journey.

The frightened Seminole continued to paddle, stroke after stoke. He changed his course more than once to create a zigzag pattern in hopes of concealing his escape. Finally Osci directed his canoe toward the east, across the water to the land of dunes and sea. Even with the impending storm, the surface of the river was a mirrored sheet of glass. This made his paddling easier, and he believed this to be a good omen or perhaps a gift from the gods.

Fear began to creep in as, plunging his paddle into the water with his muscles burning, exhaustion overcame him. Time was growing short and he strained to see in front of him. The darkness completely enveloped the water and all surroundings as he anxiously awaited the next flash of lightning to guide his way.

The tiny bundle at his feet rested quietly, even with the explosions from the sky above. Osci sat breathless, motionless at times, knowing a sound or unnecessary motion would bring unwanted attention—as well as capture and sudden death.

Even though his arms ached as Osci strained with every muscle, there was no time for rest. He drove his paddle deep into the water, moving the sleek canoe side to side. He was a strong man of physical stature, but with this great effort, combined with the amount of adrenaline pumping through his veins, he became tired long before he normally would.

Osci dismissed the thought of weakness and searched the darkness for land. He continued to look over his shoulder, left to right, hoping to see nothing following in his wake. He knew he was going to be pursued and was deathly afraid of being caught. He did not want to imagine the consequences. *Must stay focused, must complete the journey*, were the self-motivating messages running through his mind. The plan was to come ashore at the land of dunes and sea, stay a course on foot through those dunes, and follow the North Star along the coastline as the rushing waters covered his tracks.

If the task could be accomplished, he could reach the cape's swamps and forest and lose himself with his precious bundle. Osci knew a number of tribes still hunted and fished in the area and was sure they would help him vanish forever into the forest.

With a flash, the coastline appeared and disappeared in front of him. He knew he was only a few strokes away from the first steps of his new life. He ran his canoe through the reeds and up onto the shore. Osci grabbed his bundle, clutched it to his chest, and gingerly stepped through the underbrush, being careful not to leave any tracks.

The storm seemed to have subsided, but the humidity made his skin a solid sheet of sweat as every pore of his body exploded. He could feel the wetness from his head to his toes.

He continued across the tiny strip of land heading east. Small deer scattered as he moved. The sea grass seemed to whisper to him as the wind picked up, blowing in from the sea.

Osci's senses were attuned to every sound. At one point he glanced back as his breath caught finding his greatest fear was real and very close: Fire lit the water. Torches burned in the distance, and he could see one, two boats, maybe more. Some behind him, others headed in different directions. He knew he had no time to waste as they were approaching him faster and faster, closing in on him much quickly than he had imagined.

If caught, death would be a certainty. Time was of the essence and he needed to move along at a much faster pace.

The wind blew stronger off of the ocean and lightning flashed in the distance. With heart pounding and a shortness of breath, Osci held his bundle to his chest and quickened his pace to a fast trot, still being careful not to leave any tracks to be followed by the ones who were sure to come.

CHAPTER

2

"Another beautiful morning on the Space Coast!" the announcer shouted on the radio. "Looking for a high of ninety-two degrees on this beautiful Thursday, the eighteenth of November, 2011."

I drove north along U.S. Highway 1 on my way to work, windows down, radio blaring Lynyrd Skynyrds' "Sweet Home Alabama" through the speakers. I sang along and reminisced about all the countless times I had driven this route in the past. Of course, the only reason the windows were down was because the A/C didn't work.

"Hell of a thing to have in Florida, a car without A/C," I mumbled to myself. "Shit. It's too damn hot for November."

Still, I'd rather have four months of hot weather in Florida than four crappy months in Jersey, as my dad used to say.

The ride to work was the same one I had driven for the past fifteen years, and the freaking pay was still about the same too.

Oh, there was a time when big things were planned for me. But wow, how things had changed. A budding star on the court and my extended future resting on bigger things to come later on in the newsroom. I had my sights set on being the guy to sign autographs and in my later years be the announcer who says, "At the buzzer, what a shot to win it all! Your new NBA champions are…!" Damn, ESPN would have loved me.

I hate to admit it, but I actually spent hours practicing those lines in front of the mirror, and I looked pretty damn good doing it too. That all disappeared a few years ago in an instamatic minute, along with my wife, two kids, and self-esteem.

Man, life can be funny. Time has a strange way of treating you. It can be kind to you or *take away everything important to you in the wink of an eye.* For me, well, I still haven't decided how it has treated me.

But time will tell.

At this point in my life, I should have been farther along in my career, if that's what you want to call it. Life in general has still been good to me. I mean, I still look good for my age—at least so I'm told by the bar flies I meet once in a while—and I still take pretty good care of myself too.

Clean shaven, well groomed, I hit the gym five days a week, not to walk around with a cup of coffee and chitchat, but to actually work out. I run my two miles on the beach and still surf to help clear my head when I get the chance. At six feet four inches I can still hang on the beach with the best of them, and that's with my shirt off. I know I have issues, but physically I'm not bad. My ex leaving me really scrambled my brain for a while.

Yeah, well anyway, I don't have six-pack abs, but at least it's not a keg like most guys I know my age. Once in a while I still also shoot some hoops. But it always brings back bad memories, and I am really not into that. I've learned self-pity sucks, and I'd rather not go there.

I've also been told I need to age gracefully. "Tucker," my Nan would say, "you're not getting any younger, my dear." I say bullshit to that! Not me. I am not going down without a fight. I'll even get a nip and tuck if I have to. Remember, fifty is the new thirty, and sixty is the new forty. It all sounds pretty good to me.

I really do need to get this A/C fixed somehow. But hey, it's November and it can't stay hot forever. The hurricane season is just winding down, though the heat still blows in when you least expect it.

"I'll get it fixed in the spring," I mumble to myself.

Sure I will. I've been planning for the last five years to get it done, but still don't want to pay the cash to do it.

I'm a sports reporter for the local rag, and my newspaper building is just off U.S. 1 in an old section of Cocoa. Might as well be in an old section, as the building is as old as the county of Brevard. It's the oldest active daily paper in the area. The circulation isn't much anymore, but as they say, we try harder.

Our staff is small, just a few full-time reporters, and rumors of us being swallowed up by *Florida Today* have always come and gone. But hell, who really buys papers these days anyway? Even I get my news off the web.

It's my secret and I don't want anyone to know about it.

I turned into the long, narrow drive and parked my 1998 Jeep Cherokee in its usual spot under a large palm and cracked the windows just enough to keep the air moving and rain out, as the usual pop-up thunderstorms were expected later on in the day. I didn't lock it, because to be honest, there is nothing to steal. The only threat was maybe finding some bum sleeping in it, like the time I was down at Captain Hiram's on the fourth of July for a concert and drink fest. The bum ended up being a pretty cool guy, and after we both sobered up a little, I actually gave him a ride home.

The *Brevard Daily* marquee was missing the letter "r" from its place, as it had for the past eight years. So everyone actually started calling us *Bevard Daily*. Guess people think it sounds pretty funny, but I still don't get it.

The building was quiet and the lighting kept dim to cool the place. They say we're going green, but I say someone's pocketing the extra green. All I know, it's not in my pocket.

Damn, I could use that extra green. Child support was killing me.

As I entered, the usual folks were in their usual places. The everyday smiles and hellos were exchanged and

I continued to my office—or should I say cubicle. I made one pit stop—to check out what Clair was wearing. Glad I did, because checking her out in the morning was worth the price of admission. Short skirt, high heels, and a great body for a thirty-nine-year-old divorcee with two kids. Her long blonde hair cascaded around her face, and she had a smile that would light up the sky. We exchanged our usual glances, my nod and her smile. She whispered, "Are we still on this weekend?"

"Of course," I said. "Same time as usual."

She smiled and nodded her head. Clair was great. She had helped me through some pretty rough times a while back.

A little ride down A1A to Lou's Blues for some rhythm and blues with a workout between the sheets afterwards seemed like a good idea this weekend since it wasn't my weekend with the kids.

I entered my office, sorry, cubicle with the sign *Sports Editor* taped to the wall. Damn, sports editor, who were they kidding? I was the only person who covered sports and it was all local. "Remember," the boss told me, "we are a local paper," and local entailed high school and local community sports only.

This was my purgatory. High school and recreational sports, no coverage of college or pros. That was our policy.

It may sound like I bitch a little about my job, but I really can't complain too much. Money does suck, but there's no real pressure on me to win any kind of journalistic awards.

I did my usual.

Checked my messages…none! "I am so damn important."

Checked the local wire for any high school scores… no surprises there.

Got up and got a cup of coffee and looked at the opening high school hoops schedule.

Which game should I cover tomorrow on opening night?

"Decisions…decisions!"

Maybe I'd see Melbourne Independent play Rockledge in their last game scrimmage. That could be a good one and I'd get a chance to see my old coach and the hottest prospect in the Central Florida area, Mr. Everything from Melbourne. UCF, Florida, and Georgia Tech were a small part of the contingent after this kid. I'd take a good look at him and see for myself if the kid could actually play with me as Coach told me the other day!

From the corner of my eye, I noticed Mitch approaching. I pretended not to see him. Not that Mitch was a bad guy; he was just one of those guys who wanted to be everyone's friend. A nice guy, as well as small and chunky and going bald. The kind of guy who was always picked last in gym class but never got his feelings hurt because all he cared about was to just be around and hang with the "athletic guys." Plus Mitch was a hell of a nice guy, good editor, and boss.

"Hey, Tucker, how ya doing this morning?"

I took a long sip of my now cold coffee and didn't answer right away. I heard somewhere that a long pause made for a nice effect when dealing with people and questions as it apparently made you look smart. What the freak, who was I kidding?

"Hi, Mitch, what's shaking?" I smiled.

"Oh, not a hell of a lot. I've got two things for ya. First of all, I'm having a get-together this weekend on my little sailboat and wanted to know if you'd stop by? We'll stay docked, so you won't get sick," he laughed.

Yeah, that's me, the token jock, with a touch of motion sickness. Really it wasn't that bad and only happened once when we were out in the ocean with huge swells. But Mitch liked to joke about it and never let me forget it. Hell, I even have my own little Whaler to zip around the river with, and that causes me no problems at all.

Mitch seemed to think having me around helped him rise in athletic stature among many of his friends. *Look*, people would say, *Mitch must be a jock too.*

I smiled and played along, "You'll keep that thing tied up?"

"Sure will. I wouldn't want my best bud puking all over the stern," he said and obnoxiously laughed again. Yeah, okay, best bud. With his salary, he had a yacht, not a little sailboat as a toy, and I lived in a fucking trailer! I would never begrudge him his wealth, but heck; his family has owned the paper for the past seventy years or so.

What the hell, free beer and food were worth the couple hours of agony of being asked to retell for the thousandth time my best moments in sports. Plus, as bad as Mitch looked, his wife was a nice little piece to look at. Who says money can't buy you happiness or even sex, for that matter? All that he had because of his family ties to the media markets and its wealth derived from the newspaper business. All in all, Mitch really was a nice guy with a heart as big as an evening Florida sunset.

"Sure, I'd love to come by, I'll be there." It never hurt to kiss a little ass when the opportunity presented itself, especially if it's the boss's ass!

Mitch stood there and looked lost in thought.

"So Mitch, what was that number two you mentioned?" I regretted that question the moment I asked it.

"Oh yeah, almost forgot, Herb is out, think he has the flu or some shit."

Herb was our one and only investigative reporter. His investigations usually never got any bigger than why Aunt Mabel's cat down in Palm Bay got stuck in a tree, and how, after dialing 911, the fire department was there for the rescue.

"So with him laid up, and you being my go-to guy in the clutch, I need you to check out a story for us over on the beachside. It's not earth shattering, kind of a follow up to the Ed Ventara case a few years back."

Whoa there, a red light went off in my head, let me think here!

Shit, wasn't that the serial killer guy who got convicted a few years back for killing five children, even though they only found four bodies?

"You want *me to* check out that case? Mitch, don't you think it's a little out of my league?"

"Aw, don't sweat it, for you, it's like making two foul shots to win it with no time left, a piece of cake."

Great, another sports analogy from my *Best Bud*. Here he goes again. The un-jock trying to talk like one. That drives me nuts coming from a guy like Mitch. Piece of cake, my ass, bullshit, he had no idea what shooting two foul shots was like to win a game. He couldn't even hit the damn backboard if he tried.

"Uh, I don't—"

"I need you on this one, bud. They found a small skeleton on the beachside, and I need ya to go over there and check it out. Poke around and see if it's related to the others. Call me after you talk to a few sheriff's deputies, I'm sure it's an open and shut case."

Okay, I thought to myself, *beachside! I know a few good bars over there and it sounds like an easy assignment.*

I smiled. "Well, Mitch, if you really need me, you know I'm always a team player." That was pure bullshit, but he always ate it up, like we were playing for the Dolphins or something.

"Good man, I knew I could count on you. Call me when you get done and don't forget this weekend, it should be a hell of a good time." He walked away with a smile.

Well, let's see, it's ten thirty a.m., I can take the Merritt Causeway over and check out the scene. Then by let's say... twelve thirty, I can have a nice liquid lunch over at P.J.'s Riverfront Bar and Grill.

I took another sip of my now cold coffee and almost spit it out. Boy was I moving up in the world! I laughed to myself, grabbed my keys, and headed out for my first investigative reporting gig.

CHAPTER

3

The earliest inhabitants in what is now called Brevard County came to the Indian River region over twelve thousand years ago. Many societies sprang up along the Indian Lagoon and the Banana and St. Johns rivers as well as the surrounding areas, living off the abundance of the natural resources.

The Indian River region remained largely unsettled by the white man until the United States Army and Florida Militia established supply posts throughout the area during the Second Seminole War of 1837. A fort was established on a narrow strip of land now called Merritt Island. Fort Ann was a small fort, but it served as an important link and depot for supplies as more settlers came to the region.

The conflict with the Seminoles slowly eased into a stalemate, and the remaining tribes went into hiding in the Everglades and its northern extension. But many still continued expanding their hunting grounds toward the Indian River Lagoon area. Pioneers trickled into the region during the 1840s and 1850s as families started to settle in the area and harvested the natural abundance of citrus. Land was plentiful, and many grabbed up as much as they could.

By 1860, a few large plantations had popped up along the Indian River. With the impending storm brewing in the North, many of the men of the area were recruited into Confederate service to serve proudly and died for the Southern cause. During those years, a shortage of manpower made the upkeep and harvest of crops a difficult task for the remaining white men, women, and slaves.

CHAPTER

4

I headed to the beachside. The traffic on Route 520 was backed up and crowded as usual. What a change from when I was a kid. The drive through Merritt Island toward the causeway should have taken me about ten or fifteen minutes. But, of course, at this time of day, it was more like fifty minutes.

The car dealerships and Merritt Square Mall were all still the same as they were years ago, but now the addition of every fast food joint and chain restaurant you could think of crowded the landscape. The area, which was once so simple when I was a kid, with less crowds and more trees, had now become the typical congested, jam-packed shopping area that all of Florida's main roads had become since that funny little mouse arrived in Orlando some forty years ago.

No planning seemed to have gone into this mess. At least over in Viera they set up a nice square to shop in. It was classy and organized with wide roads, colored walkways, shops, restaurants, and majestic palms. It showed what a little planning could do. It was kind of like a place you'd see in California, at least the parts I'd seen depicted on TV.

Finally the traffic opened up a bit. I beat the light at Cape Canaveral Hospital and made good time up to A1A. Outside Ron Jon's Surf Shop, I made a right and headed south as the traffic started picking up again. The four-lane highway cleared a bit as soon as I hit old Cocoa Beach town center, where the north and south lanes are separated by various businesses. I passed the fire station and town hall and continued until A1A merged back into four lanes.

Farther down, the road opened up to a nice beachside roadway with its condos, restaurants, and simple homes. I continued until I came to a Mexican restaurant and turned left onto the side street. Not a lot of action here for a suspected murder scene as there was years ago at the cape when the first body of Ed Ventara's victims was discovered. Just the usual crime scene crew, a few sheriff cars, the CIU, and a couple of local reporters, none of whom I knew.

Up on the dunes, yellow tape roped off the area where deputies stood guard, and a number of people with *CIU* written across their shirts worked inside a circular area. I spotted a very old friend on the force who I had known since childhood, hanging out in plain clothes.

"Hey, Tucker, long time no see."

"How ya doin', Craig? Family good?" We shook hands and did the half man hug. That was something I still didn't get, but what the heck.

Craig was a good guy. We had played against each other a number of times in various sports throughout our pre-high school careers. Later we attended the same high school, and our rivalry developed into a mutual respect and friendship only teammates achieve. We became best friends, and the friendship grew to the point where Craig was one of the ushers in my wedding.

We remained friends despite his first wife, Debbie, being a close friend of my ex. As life has it, our careers and family took off in different directions and we only saw each other occasionally in our travels throughout town. Once in a while we'd meet over a beer...okay, three or four beers, to reminisce about the glory days. Despite a few personal problems of his own that he had to endure—though none worse than mine—he continued to work his way up the ranks in the sheriff's department. He was currently assigned to the criminal investigation unit.

"So Tuck, what brings you over here? No game going on in this area?" He laughed.

The sun shone intensely, and even with the slight breeze off the ocean, it was still warm. To the west you could see the thunderheads already heating up in the Orlando area.

"Nah, Craig, no game. I'm filling in for a co-worker who's a little under the weather. Not really doing the kind of reporting I'd like to do, but a guy's gotta eat. Can you give me a little info on what we got here?"

"Yeah, I don't see why not," Craig yawned. He looked over his shoulder toward the beach and took me by the arm as we walked away from the rest of the crowd.

"Seems this kid who's down here on vacation with his family was playing Frisbee up on the beach and winged it into the dunes. I should have given the little shit and his parents a summons for being up there. Anyway, he locates the Frisbee in some underbrush and gets his foot punctured by something in the sand. Damn if it doesn't turn out to be a bone sticking out. So, to make a long story short, here we are."

As I shaded my eyes from the afternoon glare, I looked toward the dunes, then back at Craig. "Don't mind me asking, but rumor has it this is the last of Ventara's work?"

"Yeah, could be or should be," replied Craig. "We'll determine all that official stuff later. We have no other missing persons reports for children to go on, plus the remains are small, same size and description as Ventara's last victim, the one that was never recovered years ago."

Poor kid! Ed Ventara was one of the worst serial killers to have operated in the Central Florida area. All his victims were under the age of three, and they had been abducted from right under their parents' noses. The parents, in many cases, had been out shopping and taken their eyes off their kid for just a second, and before you knew it, they were gone. Seems he was so sick, it was all just a game and a thrill for him to see the anguish in the family members' faces as they suffered over their losses. Someone should have taken it upon himself to put a few bullets into each part of his body so the bastard would suffer like those children and families did.

"Hmm...they're pretty sure of it?"

Craig pulled up his belt—he had put on a few pounds over the years—and said, "Yeah, CIU will finish up and the usual tests will be done by the medical examiner's office to be sure. Results will be back in a bit, probably Monday. I'll let you know what the outcome is if you'd like."

"That would be great, Craig, I'd really appreciate it. Is Karla still over at the examiner's office?" She was a girlfriend of Craig's the last I heard.

"Yeah, she is. I'll give her a shout in a day or two to get the info."

"Oh." I was a little surprised by the way he answered. "Not much going on with her anymore?"

"Nah," he said, "that ended a while ago, but we're still pretty good friends."

Damn, that was too bad for him. Karla was one of the prettiest and brightest women I had seen him go out with. We always joked that no matter how good a woman looked, there was always someone, somewhere, tired of putting up with her sh..., well you know the word.

We shook hands again, double checked our cell phone numbers, and I mentioned we'd get together for a drink sometime so we could reminisce about the glory days.

With everything agreed on, I returned to my car. The heat was oppressive as I started her up and had to look like an idiot with open windows. Two kids walking with their surfboards looked at me with quizzical faces as I pulled out.

I yelled, "I like the fresh air," and drove off.

I headed back toward Cocoa Beach on my way to P.J.'s. Writing a short blurb for the paper would be no big deal. I figured I could bang it out, hand it over to Mitch, and be done with it. At least I'd be able to go back to doing what I did best—sports, drinking, and women.

The report would probably hold us over until Herb returned from his illness, so I picked up my cell phone and gave Mitch a call. There was no answer, so I left a message as I turned the Jeep north on A1A and headed out.

CHAPTER

Osci paddled his canoe along the creek leading into the Indian River. His ancestors had hunted and fished in this area for as long as the stars had shined. For the first twelve years of his life, he had come to this area with his papa to hunt. For the last eight years, he had come to the area alone to enjoy the peace and tranquility. He always returned home a few days later with alligator skins and fresh deer meat. He loved the area, especially the "finger" of land that divided the two rivers from each other, as well as the land of dunes and sea farther toward where the sun rose. The land here was narrow and had an abundance of fruit trees to enjoy.

With the white man now in the area, although Osci did not perceive them as a threat, he was always careful to avoid any contact with them. He had heard stories about the horrible beatings and torture that came from the white man's hands during the days of the Seminole War, but he was no fool; he knew all men, whether white or red, were capable of violence. He did, however, find the customs and habits of the white men to be amusing.

When things were boring and hunting was at a lull, Osci would walk quietly to the edge of the white man's compounds and watch. He found the clothing the people wore quite unusual for an area as hot and sticky as this was for most of the year. He saw the handling of horses with leather coverings, or saddles as he heard them called, also a bit strange. One thing he could not understand was why so many black men let themselves be bossed around by the whites. But overall he was impressed by the grounds and the harvesting of the fruits: oranges, mangos, grapefruit, and pineapples.

On one return trip to the lagoon region, he noticed an absence of white men. The pace of life in the white man's compounds had seemed to slow, and he noticed many of the black men were missing. The women had now taken up the chores and even rode on horses to work the grounds. Old, friendly Indians from other tribes in the area helped in exchange for small metal objects called coins or for food or supplies.

That's when Osci spotted *her* coming toward him along the trail. A woman on horseback. His heart stopped, and his breathing became shallow. Though she was a white woman, she had the features common to the women of his tribe. Her cheekbones lifted her face and gave prominence to her deep blue eyes that looked down over a delicately shaped, petite nose. Her hair was long and black, but not fully black. When the sun hit her hair, a tinge of red was brought out and mixed the colors. He could not believe what he saw as she passed. He had never seen a woman with such beauty.

In the following days and weeks, Osci returned to the area, not to hunt, but to lie in wait for a glimpse of this beautiful woman. All he could think of and hope to see was this vision of loveliness.

One quiet afternoon as he watched the woman working her horse toward him, she did not pass him as she followed along the usual trail. This time she slowed her horse to a walk, stopped, and slowly dismounted. She led her horse down a narrow path toward a small body of water—on the same path that Osci was on! As she approached Osci's hiding place, she stopped, turned, and looked directly toward the brush where he lay. Osci froze in shock. His heart skipped a beat and beads of sweat formed on his brow as he wondered, *Can she see me?*

How could she?

But she did! She held her horse by the reins and took a step toward him, and to his surprise, she smiled.

Yes, smiled!

It was then he realized she knew he was there all those times before. From that moment, Osci's life was changed forever.

CHAPTER

6

Stopping at P.J.'s for my liquid lunch was just what I needed. It's a little out of the way, just off the causeway and down along the river, a great location providing the ideal atmosphere for the true Floridian. It wasn't heavily traveled and seldom found by visiting tourists. That's exactly why I liked it and tried to make it a weekly stop. The perfect escape, a place to let the world slip away for a few hours.

I turned off my cell phone and purposely left it in the car as I headed in. That was something I usually did when frequenting such an establishment; no reason to be distracted by those annoying electrical devices, which all too often ruined a man's afternoon.

The place was cool, even with the ninety degrees-plus heat outside. The windows were open to take advantage of the crossing breeze, and the ceiling fans were in full mode. It was obviously another place trying to fit into the new green mentality. Most of the barkeeps I knew had a warm smile and beer ready when I arrived. I thought it was a sure sign of friendliness and good business management, while others could say I frequented those joints way too often. Regardless, they always made me feel welcome when I pulled up a seat.

No need to read the menu, I knew it by heart. I ordered the fried calamari with a bowl of clam chowder. It's the perfect combination to go along with a cold draft beer on this hot afternoon.

The place was a little slow with no one at the bar except the bartender, Andy. He brought me my beer and came over to chat for a bit. Andy, like so many good bartenders, is more like a therapist. The things this man must know and hear. I bet he could write a book. He has enough material on me alone to do it.

"Hot as hell out there for November, Tuck," yawned Andy.

"Yes, it is, my barman. How's business today?" I said as I shook his hand.

I knew how business was, slow but steady, as usual. Andy had resettled from up north—just like every other person you meet in Florida who are all transplanted from someplace else. He had owned this tavern for about ten years now. The simple fact is he was fun to argue the sports news with, enough reason to make P.J.'s my favorite dwelling to kick back and relax.

"So you going up to Gainesville for the season tip-off?" Andy sneered. He knew I wasn't, he just wanted to bust my chops.

"Nah, we have enough excitement right here in good old Brevard to keep me on my toes." Plus the idea of watching a college team play, especially one I had a full ride to many years ago, before I blew out my knee, was not something I wanted to do.

I'll admit it. I'm still stuck on what "could have been" rather then what "is." At times I feel I'm getting better with it, but damn, it's been haunting me for so long. I whined a lot about it in the past, and I even took time to see a therapist, without any luck. I also believe it probably had a little to do with my divorce. Okay, who am I kidding! It had a lot to do with my divorce. Even though I did play at a small school in Saint Augustine, I was stuck in limbo for such a long time and couldn't get over what could have been for me at the big school. Don't get me wrong, playing in Saint Augustine for four years was enjoyable, but after the knee, being a step slower with no vertical leap, the promised calls that would have come from the NBA after four years at a big D1 school never materialized.

"That's great, Tuck, glad to see you're on top of the local stuff." Andy smiled with a gleam in his eye that showed he got me.

"Really, there's a lot of good ball being played here. You should check it out sometime," I smirked back.

Andy just grinned and went to wait on a couple of locals who walked through the door.

After watching ESPN and chowing down on my lunch and another beer, it was time to hit the road. I threw twenty-five bucks on the counter, called out a friendly good-bye to Andy, who smiled and saluted, and headed out the door.

The shade had started to creep across the parking lot and a breeze had picked up. It looked like a front was approaching, so hopefully things would cool down.

I got in the Jeep and fired the old girl up. I figured I'd head back to the office to write a short blurb for the case and be done with it, then head home and see what game the sports channel had on to watch. Also, stopping at the office now would guarantee the avoidance of Mitch, since I knew he skipped out early every Thursday and Friday.

I picked up my cell, turned it back on, and saw there were four missed calls with voice mails. Boy was I popular! I really didn't want to listen while I was driving, so I figured it could wait until I got back to the office to check them out. My messages were usually not too important, so what the hell, they could wait. As I left the parking lot, I had the unusual feeling I was being watched. I looked around, saw nothing, and just chalked it up to my wild imagination at work again.

CHAPTER

Getting back to the office took a little longer than normal. U.S. 1 was backed up, which was usual for this time of day, and the railroad crossing rail was stuck down, which wasn't usual, but wasn't uncommon. I could feel a drop in the temperature, and the sky was taking on the dark copper color that usually meant a storm was imminent.

As expected, when I got to the office everyone was gone, except for the janitorial crew and a few evening staff workers. Nice and quiet. It should only take me about ten to fifteen minutes to post my report for Mitch to edit, and I'd be out the door.

I picked up my office mail and checked my voice messages on the office phone. Nothing. As they say, no news is good news.

Oops, I just remembered I had to check the messages on my cell phone.

Beep #1: "Tucker, it is now the eighteenth of the month and your child support was due on the first of the month. I am sick and tired of reminding you of your responsibilities. Get your shit together or I'll have my lawyer go to family court and get your pay garnished." Marion laughed. "Pay, if that's what you call it...And another thing, you low—"

Beep, message deleted. I had heard enough of that bitch's voice.

I can't believe she busts my chops about child support, I thought. *I really don't mind supporting my kids, but damn, she re-married well. I bet my child support goes to pay the household staff rather than my kids.*

Beep #2: "Hey, Tucker, just thought I'd give you a call and let you know I was thinking of you. Hope your day at the beach went well." She laughed. "Be good— see ya." Clair was a doll. A great catch for someone. I just didn't feel I was the guy who should be caught or in any relationship. Plus, if you combined my baggage with hers—four teenagers and whacked-out exes—it was not a situation I needed right now. But she had a great body and was fantastic in bed, can't deny her that!

Beep #3: "Hey, buddy, it's Mitch. Hope you made out well today. Listen, I want you to do a bang-up job on your report. I heard the other papers are not going to give Ventara anymore headline coverage, so I need you to do me a big favor and do it up right."

Oh no, here it comes. I hate the words *favor* and *right* in the same sentence.

"Tuck, I need you to interview Ventara."

What the fuck?

"I already arranged it for you, I called in a few favors, a close friend owes me…"

Son of a bitch!

"Shoot up to Raiford Prison tomorrow and spend some quality time with Ventara. Enjoy the day and I'll see you at the party," he finished with a laugh. I deleted his message. I couldn't freaking believe it! Why me? And on a Friday, shit.

Beep #4: "…and another thing you lowlife, I can't trust you to do—"

Deleted. Thanks, Marion, I feel the exact same way about you.

I knew tomorrow was not going to be an enjoyable day. The ride alone was a pain in the ass, especially with every weekend warrior flying up and down Interstate 95.

It was now going to be an early night, so I grabbed a few things for my morning road trip and headed out the door toward home for some early shuteye.

CHAPTER

8

Tucker found himself watching as the shadow of an Indian moved slowly through the darkness and mist. Flashes of lightning spotted the sky. The shadow appeared lost, in need of help and guidance. It had been on a journey for so long and now had come its chance to finally put things to rest, rest that would be forever and peaceful.

The Indian stood alone in the darkness and began to walk—no, float—slowly over the water and grasslands. Tucker became entranced, feeling he had no choice but to follow the Indian. He found himself staying close to the Indian as they drifted through the darkness. Tucker looked to the sky and watched the flashes of lightning as stars still sparkled despite the storm.

The air became stiflingly humid. Tucker could hardly breathe. The vision led Tucker down a path that led out of the water and through the brush to a trailer. It was Tucker's trailer.

The door was open and they both entered. Darkness prevailed as they glided toward the bedroom.

As they entered the bedroom, Tucker could see himself asleep and the Indian hovering over his motionlessness body. He didn't move, he didn't talk, all he did was stand over Tucker's sleeping body and stare with his head hanging down and arms outstretched.

The Indian slowly raised his head and turned toward Tucker as his expression pleaded for help. Tucker froze as the eyes of the apparition turned crimson red as he kept his face fixed in Tucker's direction.

* * *

Tucker awoke from the dream with a clap of thunder. It shook the trailer and lit up the room. He saw a shadow at the end of his bed, and in an instant it was gone. He slowly sat up and tried to control his breathing as the room alternated between light and dark.

Tucker was drenched; sweat was dripping from every pore in his body. For the first time in a very long time, Tucker was scared. He wiped his eyes and switched on the tabletop lamp.

Wow, what a nightmare. It felt so real!

Tucker hadn't had a nightmare or anything like it in an exceedingly long time. He got up and changed his shirt then took a quick visit to the bathroom to wet his face. He felt like a child again as he walked through the trailer making certain the doors were locked and nothing was lurking under the bed or in the closets.

"Crap, what the hell am I, eight years old?" he muttered to himself. He literally shook, as if he was trying to knock the cobwebs from his brain.

After a thorough check of his surroundings, Tucker chalked it up to just being a weird dream. Still, he found it difficult to stop thinking about those eyes and the deep red glow that had penetrated his thoughts. At times he tended to over-think things, looking for reasons for what happened, but after some thought he found no hidden meaning in this experience.

He returned to bed with images of the dream still fresh in his mind. It was all so vivid, and the feeling of actually being there felt all too real. Tucker got himself comfortable as he continued to check the shifting shadows in his room for any unusual movement. His eyes grew heavy and sleep found him once again as the storm rolled off to the south.

CHAPTER

9

After a restless night thanks to that bizarre dream, I headed out early for my journey to the northern part of the state.

I started my faithful Jeep, rolled out of my carport, and glided down the street. I gave the usual hellos and waves and stopped to wish my adopted mom, Ms. Ellie, a good morning. She was a kindly old biddy who had no close relatives to speak of and was continuously sending me plates of leftovers that I usually sent straight to the trash can. I always, however, told her later how her meals were as good as any gourmet chef could prepare.

"Good morning, Ms. Ellie," I said and smiled. "Your flowers look lovely today." Just call me Atticus Finch, I crack myself up sometimes.

"Good morning, Tucker," she answered.

"Hell of a storm we had last night." She looked at me funny, so I continued, "I couldn't believe how loud the thunder was and the way the rain pelted my awnings. Thought the place would be shaken to pieces."

Again she looked at me like I had two heads and finally said, "What storm?"

I tried to hide the tiny shudder now starting to creep up my spine. "The storm last night," I repeated.

"Why, Tucker, you crazy thing, you, don't play with an old lady's mind that way. We had no storm last night. Look around the ground, it's as dry as the Mojave Desert, you silly man."

She startled me, but she was right. The ground was as dry as a bone and the usual palm branches and other foliage that litter the ground after a big storm were missing.

"You must have had too much *fire water* last night."

She gave me a stare, only a short stare, but it sent goose bumps all over me. Red eyes looked at me and a grimace took over her tiny, lined face. The look lasted only for a moment, but the mention of fire water threw me for a loop.

"You knucklehead, you," she chuckled, and in a second everything was back to normal. Still chuckling, she turned away and continued to tend to her plants.

I decided that maybe I was losing it with the dream and all and decided to forget about it. I waved good-bye and blew her a kiss. She caught it and blew it back to me the way she had a hundred times before, but as I drove away and checked the rearview mirror, the strangest thing happened. For a second, for only just a quick second, I saw those unusual red eyes and a smirk on her face.

I shook myself and figured I was sleep deprived and seeing things.

The ride to Raiford Prison would take me about three hours, give or take a few minutes. I figured Interstate 95 would be more packed than usual with the approaching tourist season and the start of a beautiful weekend, so I decided to take the road less traveled, so to speak, and headed up through the heart of the state. I stopped at the corner Quick Mart, gassed up, and grabbed a coffee and donut. Okay, I grabbed two donuts, what the hell, it was a long ride.

The weather was clear as I traveled through the interior section of the state with little traffic to impede me. These were the towns the little mouse had overlooked and never spotted by the hordes of spring breakers— or any tourist for that matter. Traveling at slower than normal speed was extremely enjoyable, as I passed small ranches, palm tree farms, and even a gator farm. This was the Florida time forgot, the Florida I grew up knowing and still loved to visit.

I passed through Raiford and approached the imposing gates of the prison. Large walls ran as far as I could see in both directions, and iron gates marked the official start of the road leading onto the property. I guess that was the intent of such an entrance. Make it look like a place you wouldn't want to spend any significant time in. I was in true awe as I stared up at the enormous monogrammed entrance. Honestly, I was scared shitless at the thought of being confined between the walls of this dreadful place.

Don't get me wrong, I was no angel as a kid. I was the usual teenage boy—cutting school to surf, drinking on the beach, and chasing bikini-clad spring breakers when I shouldn't have. I was also the typical adult male; cutting work, drinking when I shouldn't, and still chasing any lovely female over the legal age, but I never caused the type of trouble that would place me behind those daunting walls.

My ex-wife would love to see me here, but I wasn't about to give her any more pleasure than I used to deprive her of when we were married. I grinned at the thought.

After I parked and made my way through the usual check point introductions that a guest at this type of facility receives, I was led to the office of Lieutenant Debra Nicholson, a tall, attractive blonde who was head of protocol for this state facility.

Her appearance caught me off guard and immediately, like so many other times with attractive females, I found myself at a disadvantage. She was as tall as a model, lean with a pretty smile, and her golden hair was tied in a tight bun atop her head. She did not look like a woman you would find working in a place like this.

"Good afternoon, Mr. Anderson," she said with a smile as I sat across from her.

"Please, call me Tucker. I still have trouble identifying with the 'mister' part." I chuckled, acting as if I was oh so suave. Damn, she was hot for a woman I would guess to be in her mid...shit, I couldn't tell.

She grinned. "Okay, Tucker, we usually don't permit such quick visitation arrangements to interview our inmates, especially ones on death row, but Mitch is a very close..." she paused as her cheeks turned a light red, "...college friend of mine, and I owe him a favor or two."

Wait! A close college friend? Don't tell me she was saying what I thought she was. No, she had to be kidding me. This immediately threw my mind into a jumble. No way had she had that type of relationship with Mitch! I mean, look at her...and look at Mitch! Two totally different ends of the spectrum. No way...nah...couldn't have.

She continued, "Since Mitch told me you and he are buddies, I'm sure he told you we were pretty serious back in the day, at FSU."

That's it. You're freaking kidding me here. No way! I stared at her, dumbfounded, and my mouth must have been hanging open to my knees.

She went on, "I need to fill you in on our inmate Mr. Ventara. Because of the short notice, you'll have only ten minutes to speak with him and then he'll be taken back to his cell, no additional time. A heads-up for you Mr...Tucker, Mr. Ventara is not, as you say, a very credible source. Even though he is waiting to commute his sentence and believes he has a clear conscience, he still can't be trusted with anything he may say or do. Just something I think you should keep in mind."

I sat and nodded my head like a little child, but I probably heard only half of what she said. I was still in awe of the fact she and Mitch had spent some quality time together in college. What a horrible vision. Certainly not of her, but of Mitch.

"Thank you, Lieutenant Nicholson, Mitch and I appreciate everything you're doing for us today," *and I'm sure what you did for him back in the day*, I said to myself. Shit, he was a lucky bastard.

We shook hands and I was escorted out. My mouth must have still been hanging open to my knees because she smiled and had that knowing look all females get when they know they've caught you totally off guard. Damn it, why did this always seem to happen to me?

It was a long, cold walk to the visitation area, and it made me realize that if they wanted, you could easily disappear in here and never get out from behind these walls.

I sat in my temporary ten-minute home, a small cubicle with the stereotypical partition between me and the empty seat across, soon to be filled with a serial killer.

The door on the opposite side of the room opened. A guard came in and stepped aside. He was followed by a short, gray-haired man who could have passed for someone's granddad. Another guard followed and closed them into the small room.

His skin was pale against the bright orange prison garb. His features were pronounced, with a long, pointy nose and dimpled chin. Even though his hair had turned a shade of gray, an absence of wrinkles kept his age a mystery. The one characteristic that caught me by total surprise was his eyes. Black, dark black pupils with an eerie stillness in them. They were knowing eyes, having the ability to cut right through you.

He stood for a very long moment just staring at me. He just stood there and appraised his new surroundings, waiting for me to acknowledge him and invite him to sit down. I finally gave him a grin

He sat down and I picked up the receiver. "Mr. Ventara, my name is Tucker Anderson, and I'm a reporter with the *Brevard Daily*. I was hoping I could have a moment to ask you a few questions."

"A moment?" He chuckled. "Life is full of moments that pass in an instant; you pick and choose the ones important to you."

What the hell kind of answer was that?

"I absolutely agree with you, Mr. Ventara." I figured I'd go with whatever he said and hopefully he'd feel comfortable talking with me, even though I hadn't a clue what the hell he meant. He just stared at me with those black eyes. A few minutes passed without me even realizing the time.

"So, Mr. Anderson, what brings you to this lovely retreat?" he finally said. I thought about telling him to call me Tucker, but fuck him, I didn't want to be on a first name basis with this animal.

"I just wanted to confirm some information that has come to light about your...uh, your..."

"My past indiscretions?"

"Yes, if you want to call them that," I replied.

"Well, go ahead, Mr. Anderson, fire away."

"Yesterday, the remains of a small child were found on the beachside, just south of Cocoa Beach, and we believe, or should I say the authorities believe, them to be the remains of your last victim. Can you confirm or deny the information for me, and would you also like to make any kind of statement with regards to it?"

This was old news; the crimes committed by Ed Ventara happened four years ago. The other news agencies would give this story no more than a blurb inside their interior pages. That's what Mitch was hoping for, and by writing an investigative follow up, hopefully our circulation would pick up a bit, especially with it being a local crime.

"Mr. Anderson, I heard about the discovery on the news yesterday, and I'm actually surprised anyone came up to talk to me," he said. "What leads everyone to believe this is my last victim?"

"According to the investigators, your cold case is the last unsolved missing child case in the area," I answered.

"Well, tell me, Tucker, did you see the crime scene?" His face lit up. "And were the remains found in a dune?"

Wait a minute, I was the one who was supposed to be asking the questions, but I'd go with this and see where Ventara was headed. I nodded.

"Hmm," he sighed, "Mr. Anderson, I have a news flash for you and everyone else. I did not place the remains of my last victim in a dune."

I froze for a second. This confession, if you could call it one, caught me off guard. He went on. "I have nothing to hold back right now, my fate is sealed, and I have no reason to lead you on. So, Mr. Anderson, I'm being very frank with you."

"Wait, Mr. Ventara," I started, "I can quote you with that statement?"

"Absolutely!"

"Well, if that's not…"

"The remains I left then whose are they?" he went on. "All I can say, Mr. Anderson, is it's not one of my precious treasures. Mine is resting in peace, where he will never be found or disturbed."

The asshole was starting to eat at me. "Tell me, Ventara, did you see the pain in the family's eyes when the camera scanned them at the memorial?"

"How I miss those moments," he answered with a smile.

"You son of a bitch"

A guard walked over and said, "Time to go, Ed."

As Ventara raised his slight frame off of his seat to leave, he coolly smirked and added, "As for the mystery of whose remains they are, that's for you to figure out. You're the investigative reporter here, Mr. Anderson."

I could only hope that this asshole would feel the pain as his life was taken from him during his approaching scheduled execution.

He hung up the receiver and walked toward the door, escorted by the two guards. In the last instance before he cleared the door, he looked back at me, and again it sent chills down my spine. There, in his eyes and on his face, if only for a second, were the same red glowing eyes and sneer I saw on Ms. Ellie's face that morning.

CHAPTER

10

I took the fastest route out of Raiford and hit Interstate 95 in no time at all. It wasn't as enjoyable as the morning ride, but it was faster. I wanted to get back to my favorite pastime, a basketball game, so I needed to haul ass. Time flew by, mainly because of the repetitive words playing over again in my head uttered by Ventara: *It's not the body of my last victim. My precious treasure will not be found or disturbed.*

So if it wasn't a Ventara victim and Craig told me there were no cold cases involving children left to search for, then whose remains were they?

This played in my mind. Ventara had to be lying; Lieutenant Nicholson told me not to believe a word he said.

Oh, what the heck, probably some bureaucratic screw up by someone who got the case information wrong. Anyway, it wasn't my business or problem. I'd hand it all over to Mitch, and Herb could figure it out when he got back to work. I'd get back to sports, drinking, and the occasional woman or two.

I stayed on I-95 making good time down past Daytona, until I reached the Melbourne exit an hour later. It was now five thirty, and the tip-off of the Melbourne vs. Rockledge game was an hour off. So I zipped along Eau Gallie and turned right on Wickham to grab a bite to eat.

My arrival at the high school a little while later brought back so many memories. It was here that I played a man's game at a very young age. The county school district had done a fantastic job on the new construction they completed a year ago, and it would be my first visit to the complex. The changes to the campus amazed and saddened me at the same time.

Gone was the old field house with its exhaust fans that had been there since the place opened, way before air conditioning. The entrance hallway with all the photos of previous high school greats had vanished. The parquet wooden floor with its soft spots that would disrupt the visitors' dribble had been replaced. And finally, gone were its soft, friendly rims always giving the home team an advantage. It wasn't quite the same.

I did, however, have to give credit to the school board for having the foresight to keep the building of the new modern gymnasium in their plans when the budget was trimmed.

As I entered the newly renovated complex, I was pleasantly surprised. What it lacked in character, it made up with all the greater high-tech comforts all the other school lacked. I noticed they kept most of the memorabilia from the old gym. The "wall of fame," or should I say the "wall of shame," which I have called it since my picture was put up there, had all the photos of the past one thousand point scorers. A banner listing all conference and state players was hanging at one end. Seeing my name always felt good. Another wall was decorated with the various records held by the male and female legends of seasons past.

I took a moment to reflect on past glory days and headed into the gym. The place was packed for opening night and both teams were in the middle of their warm ups.

I headed to the home stands, and Coach Elderly caught my eye and had a smile running from ear to ear. Coach was in his thirtieth season, his last year, for the fifth year in a row. He told me numerous times I would be the one to force him into early retirement when I played because I aggravated him so much. He, on the other hand, became a major influence in my life, along with his wife who kept me on track. They praised me when I did well, yet both were strict enough to kick me in the ass when I didn't.

"Good to see you, son." He smiled.

Coach had taken on the role of my surrogate father. I was only thirteen when the police came to Nana's house to give her the bad news. My dad had been out on his boat that day; they said there was a horrible explosion and no remains or cause could be found. Up until that point, Dad was my world, playing the role of two parents in the absence of my mother who had disappeared from my life when I was four. It took me a long time to get over his loss, and I'm still not sure I have. It was then all left up to Nana. Don't get me wrong, she was great and really loved me, but I was a young boy full of energy she simply couldn't match. She's the one who finally introduced me to Coach and forced me to stay active in sports. She wouldn't stand for any of my self-pity. So as an overactive high school teenager, Coach became the disciplinarian I desperately needed.

I smiled and gave him a long hug before sitting down, telling him we would talk later.

The game was a blowout, and I snuck out in the third quarter before I had a chance to talk to Coach and "Mr. Everything." The kid that every college was interested in did impress me. He had good size, handle, and could drain the three from way behind the arc. Kind of reminded me of myself before...well, before everything fell apart.

The ride home was uneventful and the night sky had finally overtaken the day. Traffic lights glistened on U.S. 1 and people seemed to be hurrying more as a prelude to the upcoming holiday shopping.

I pulled into my car port, turned off old faithful, and headed to the door. I noticed a light was on in the trailer and I was a little hesitant at first because I didn't remember leaving any on. I slowly entered, took a look around, and deemed everything okay before heading back to my bedroom.

A soft light was on Clair, accentuating her tanned, nude body with her long blonde hair hiding all the nice places.

"I've been waiting for you." Clair smiled.

I'm not usually at a loss for words, but looking at her left my mouth open and drool seeping from the sides. "I'm…I'm glad you are," I stumbled.

"I had some time to kill, so I figured I'd surprise you with some quality time before I have to get home to the kids."

It sounded good to me.

"It's been a hot day and I need a shower. You're more than welcome to join me if you'd like."

"Nah, that's okay," she answered as she waved me off. "I'll wait, so don't be long."

So after a quick shower, I was delighted to find Clair bare-assed and ready to please. I slowly slid the towel off my hips to display my appreciation to her erotic invite.

"Wow, I guess you are glad to see me." She giggled.

I just smiled.

It was a long day, so I planned on taking this slow. I started with a nice foot message as my tongue worked its way up her thighs.

She moaned. "Right there, that's the spot."

I loved how she guided my head to the rocking pressure she needed to reach her climax, but I wasn't going to give in to her that easily. I teased her for a while longer, working my hands and mouth around her beautiful body, feeling her back arch off the bed as I took her breast into my mouth. When I knew she couldn't take it anymore, I granted her wish with a smile on my face. I allowed Clair to flip me on my back, straddle my waist, and take me deep inside her as she rocked gently to the sounds of her own moans and groans—just the way she likes it.

CHAPTER

11

Tucker was in a place he did not recognize, surrounded by a shroud of mist and darkness. He wasn't sure where he was, and a feeling of uneasiness overcame him. He couldn't run, hear, or even move. Where was he? Why was he here? The mist started to abate and Tucker began to see clearly.

He was on water, and though he couldn't touch the surface, the feeling of wetness prevailed. Lightning flashed, yet there was no sound of thunder. It felt as if time was stuck in a vacuum. Tucker now had a clear view of what was in front of him, as between the flashes of lightning he saw a small canoe.

The canoe was being paddled through the glassy water by a man with broad, tanned, powerful shoulders. His hair was dark, long, and braided. Tucker couldn't make out who it was, but he knew he had to follow, and he did. He was drawn behind the canoe by a power stronger than his will.

Tucker could sense the excitement of others. As the lightning continued to flash, he could see back to the shore and noticed a number of men with torches break up into different groups, launch various boats, and start to row in different directions, all except for one group that followed the canoe.

Tucker began to feel anxious. He was caught in a position he sensed was dangerous for the man in the canoe.

The canoe in front of him was unrelenting as it slid along through the water, propelled by the man he now recognized to be an Indian, the same Indian from his previous dream. He continuously looked back toward Tucker, but not at him. His eyes looked through him with an unusual red glare as the canoe continued across the river toward the beach.

A terrified look appeared on the Indian's face as he struck land. He turned and looked past Tucker and then, unlike before, he looked directly at Tucker. Their eyes made contact. This change startled Tucker as the intense red eyes of the Indian seemed to beg him, "Follow me." The Indian bent over and picked up something that looked like a sack. Hugging it to his chest, he started through the reeds toward the beach.

The wind subsided and lightning flashed over the water. Tucker floated behind Osci as they crept along a deer path toward the dunes.

The Indian looked back again, and Tucker saw that the men who carried torches in the rowboats were closer than he realized. The Indian quickened his pace through the dunes and down toward the incoming tide. But what Tucker saw the Indian did not. Coming along the beach from both directions was a swarm of men with torches. Tucker tried to yell to the Indian, but no sound came from his mouth. He was trapped. The boat behind him unloaded and another group of men followed their path.

The Indian, with his package in hand, tried to run, but was caught at the water's edge. He fell to his knees and didn't move. Men stood over him with their torches held like spears angled at his body. They seemed to be yelling, but with the deafening sounds of the waves crashing and thunder now exploding, it was impossible for Tucker to hear what was being said.

From behind Tucker three men approached from the boat. They were led by a man, tough in appearance with a stature that implied he was a man of great importance. He wore a military jacket with the bars of a captain. He carried a torch and had a sword hanging at his side. The other men followed in a subordinate role. They passed by Tucker and stood on top of a nearby dune. The Indian was brought to his feet and dragged with his sack in hand up the dune to the waiting group.

There, words were exchanged between the waiting men while the Indian stood captive and motionless with his bundle clutched to his chest.

The men reached for his bundle, but the Indian held it tighter. A rifle butt came down hard on his head, dropping him to his knees as the bundle was ripped from his grasp and flung to the sand. A look of complete terror took hold of the Indian. His eyes widened, his mouth opened, and a shriek that Tucker could not hear but could feel came from deep within his soul. As lightning flashed, the captain held his glistening sword high in the air and quickly stroked it onto the bundle.

* * *

With a clap of thunder and flash of lightning, Tucker awoke.

"What the fuck? I'm losing my mind!" Sweat poured profusely from every pore of his body and his heart felt as if it was pounding out of his chest.

He turned to reach for Clair, but remembered she had to be home for her kids and had left a while ago.

Tucker slowly got up and looked out the window to make sure there really was a storm outside before he went to the bathroom and back to bed.

An uneasiness kept Tucker tossing and turning for the next few hours, until sleep finally came to him as the morning sun rose on a new day.

CHAPTER

12

Being Saturday and not having to rush to work, I decided to sit at my little kitchen table and gaze out the window as I tried to get my senses in touch with my surroundings. I've always had dreams, a good percentage of them enjoyable ones about sports and women. I'd try to get back to sleep for those and wished they'd continue. But these latest dreams...well, these were different. They weren't quite nightmares, but they weren't something I'd like to have again. The vision of the Indian made me feel uneasy.

The morning's coffee awakened my thoughts. The sun sliced through the palm branches, and the drop in humidity promised a warm and sunny day. It pleased me to see that along the park's roadway were a few palm branches and scattering of puddles from last night's storm. I gained a little solace from the fact that at least it did storm and it wasn't just in my mind.

But the dreams still lingered in my subconscious. It was a little strange to have the same Indian show up in them. The dreams were different, but the Indian was the same in both. I assumed he was in my family genealogy tree somewhere. Nana had always told me we had some Seminole Indian blood running through our veins. She was right, of course, but I never really gave it much thought. Hum ...maybe my great-great-ancestors were pissed at me for something? Might as well join the club. Seemed someone was always pissed at me for one thing or the other.

That brought a smile to my face, soon erased as I remembered I needed, not wanted, to call the ex back.

I looked all over for my cell phone and finally located it on the bedroom floor. There were two missed calls with messages. The first was one from Clair saying she would stop by but couldn't stay long. Obviously she had made it before she snuck into my bedroom. Oh my lovely Clair, that visit was awesome, I almost forgot about it with the weird dream last night.

The second, as I guessed, was the ex. Might as well hear this one, should make for a good morning laugh.

Beep: "Hi, Tucker, hope you get this message by tomorrow," "she said with a singsong voice.

Okay, something's up. I'd known her long enough to read her tone of voice, and it was way too sweet.

"I need you to do me a favor."

There it was again, that word I despised—favor. I never used it, that's something I took pride in, but everyone hit me with it. "Charles and I have a luncheon today over at the Regional Medical Center, and I need you to watch Jessica and Carl. Since you're their daddy," she said with a laugh, "I know you won't mind. Even though it's not your weekend, I'm sure you'd never miss an opportunity to spend time with your kids, right? We should be home by around six or so; you'll still have your evening to do…well, whatever you do with your evenings. Give me a call back in the morning, thanks, I'll owe you one."

Owe me one? No, shit. What a sweetheart she could sound like when she wanted to, and what a bitch she was most of the time.

I quickly hit the redial on the phone, got Marion's answering service, and left a quick message saying I'd be more than pleased to spend time with my kids. I always took every extra chance I could get since she screwed me over in family court and gave me only every other weekend.

I got up from the table, placed my cup into the land of unwashed dishes, showered, shaved, and headed out to pick up the kids. I figured we would take a boat ride, dock beachside for lunch, and make a day of it. The ex said they'd be home by six, still leaving me with enough time to make it over to Mitch's party.

The long-awaited front had moved through during my dream and the humidity had all but disappeared. The sun felt warm and the temperature would climb to about eighty-two degrees today. A slight breeze accompanied the temperature and made for a perfect Central Florida day.

I headed north on U.S. 1 to catch the causeway and head south on Merritt Island. I turned right on 520 and then a right on Tropical Trail. The homes in this section of Merritt were small, quaint, and blue collar. The farther south you traveled the larger and more expensive the homes became. Many were waterfront, meticulously landscaped, of the white collar variety. A few were set up on hilltops—only in Florida would these mounds of dirt be considered hills—considered the highest points in Brevard County. That's where my children now lived with their mom and step-dad doctor.

I turned onto Honeymoon Lane, with its million-dollar homes, and pulled into the biggest house on the street, with Honeymoon Lake as its back yard. I have to admit, it's a gorgeous home, as well as a great place to live and grow up in as a kid. It had a great location with views of the Indian River on one side and the Banana River on the other side, with the lake as a backdrop.

The kids were waiting and I got the customary hugs and kisses, but also the looks that said, *Do we really have to leave paradise to spend the day with you?* Carl was still young enough at nine years of age to enjoy a day with Dad, but Jessie was another story.

At fourteen, she was gorgeous and looked like she was twenty-one, with an attitude to match. Must be the water and weather here in Florida, because even when I was a kid we all seemed to mature and grow up way too fast compared to the rest of the kids I met from around the country.

"Dad, please get out of here fast, you're making us look bad in this thing you call a car," Jessie yelled as she sank down below the window. "My friends can't see me in this!"

"It's a Jeep, Jess...a *Jeep*," I retorted.

"Yeah, yeah, Dad. Whatever." God forbid if she was seen in anything less than her mother's Mercedes. Man, is she her mother's daughter or what?

We made great time back to the mainland and down U.S. 1 to my boat, which was just a short hop, skip, and a jump from my house...I mean trailer.

The air was crisp and the sun shone in abundance. Carl was excited, but Jess, of course, just followed along with a scowl on her face, IP buds stuck in her ear, texting away on her cell phone to who knows who. We jumped onto my little Whaler and prepared to cast off. I've had the Whaler, an eighteen-footer, for a number of years. It was always a good conversation piece when talking to a new female.

"I have a boat," is all I'd have to say, and their interest would be piqued. Little did they know it wasn't a yacht, but what the heck, my chances of getting lucky improved by ninety percent.

I wasn't a fisherman like my dad, but I did enjoy rides on the water, especially when I could dock up to a restaurant or bar. That was one great thing about Florida. There were just as many bars you could boat to as ones you could drive to.

I fired up the engine and off we went. A nice lunch at P.J.'s sitting on the back deck with the reggae band playing would be a nice touch for the kids—or so I thought.

I kept the boat between the channel markers and, after leaving the no wake zone, opened her up. The water was a sheet of glass as we skimmed our way across the river. When we arrived, a local crowd was there, including many I knew. The usual hellos and smiles were exchanged, and my daughter, with her shorts and bare, strapless top, got a few—no, a lot of—looks from guys of all ages. I had to stare back at them with my *who the fuck do you think you're looking at, she's only fourteen!* look.

The band was actually pretty good and played a number of renditions of Marley and Buffet. This thankfully loosened Jessie up a bit, so we exchanged updates as we waited for our order.

Carl spoke about school and some of the new friends he made at Scouts, and I promised him I'd do an activity with him in the near future. Maybe those race car derbies would be fun. He liked the idea.

Jess, on the other hand, had all the problems of any fourteen-year-old girl. Boy dramas, cliques, and tattoos were foremost on her mind.

"Tattoos?" I exclaimed. "What do you mean you're thinking of getting a tattoo? Sweetie, I don't—"

"Oh, Dad, you're so old-fashioned. All the girls are getting something. Stop being such a dork, Dad. You are so back in the dino age." Dino age!

She read the shocked look on my face and said, "Don't worry, Daddy, I don't want my first one to be anything big, just a little ankle band or bikini flower. They're so awesome."

"Your *first* one?"

I was still in shock. Women can do that to me, and now my daughter had joined the club.

Carl just sat munching on some chips, oblivious to the entire conversation. He could care less what his sister was up to.

"When do you plan on getting this, honey?" I groaned.

"Oh, as soon as Mom gets time to take me; she needs to sign for me, ya know. That whole eighteen thing is crap. I should be able to do what I want, it's my body."

I just sat there and smiled as I thought, *I'll take care of this. Wait until I talk to that bitch of a mother.*

"She said maybe next week. She said I could go to the same shop in Cocoa Beach she went to for hers."

"She has one?" I almost choked on my iced tea, not only because of what Jess said, but also because it wasn't a beer.

We let the topic go and changed to something else. Jessie had scrambled my brain and was starting to give me a headache. I settled myself down and sat back to enjoy a little of the band as Jess went back to texting or whatever the hell she was doing on that thing.

Lunch was served, a burger for Carl, chicken sandwich for Jess, and a pulled jerk sandwich for me. At least the kids smiled as we ate, but my brain was still rattled over my conversation with Jess.

After we consumed our lunch, or should I say devoured, especially by Carl, we motored off to our next destination beachside. We set ashore a little south of Cocoa Beach and made our way across A1A to the beach.

An eerie feeling came over me as we walked along. Then it dawned on me. We were at the scene of the skeletal find. Approaching the area by boat from the river side of A1A had made me lose sight of where we were, but that's not what caught me off guard. I suddenly realized this was also the area I had experienced in my dreams. It had the same dunes and pathway I clearly remember following the Indian through. Why hadn't I figured this out sooner? Strange I would unconsciously pick this beach to go to.

We walked along the street past the Mexican restaurant and continued up to the dune crossing. Then for a second, but just for a second, I spotted something from the corner of my eye that sent chills down my spine. It was an Indian, the Indian from my dreams, and he was standing on the dune, the dune of the skeletal find, looking directly at me. He stood with outstretched arms and those eerie red eyes. In an instant, the vision was gone.

CHAPTER

13

A decade and a half before the Civil War, at Fort Brinkelton in Jacksonville, Captain Saunders of the Florida Militia became a single father, not by choice but by circumstance. He had fought and been decorated in the Seminole Wars, but what he was about to undertake was the greatest challenge he would ever have to face.

Crystal Ann Saunders was born to Captain Saunders and his wife, Martha, but in the process of giving Crystal life, Martha had passed away. As happens in many instances, Captain Saunders did not shun his newborn daughter, but rather clung to her, showering her with unconditional love and affection.

Being raised as an only child at a military fort was unusual, especially for a girl. Crystal experienced a life growing up like no other. She learned to saddle and ride her own horse, shoot a rifle, capture and skin her own pelts. Crystal was one of the troops, accepted by all of her twenty-five adopted fathers. The only female nurturing she received growing up came from Nabi, a half-black, half-Seminole woman who became Crystal's nanny shortly after her birth. A close bond developed between the two that could only be described as unique. Nabi taught Crystal many of the skills expected to be learned only by males. Many joked about Crystal becoming an Indian because of her closeness with Nabi. This wasn't entirely false since Crystal learned to respect and love the ways of the people many whites called their enemy.

As time passed, the transformation that occurs when a cocoon develops into a beautiful butterfly happened to Crystal. It happened gradually, but she blossomed into a young woman who became the object of desire for many young men. She was absolutely beautiful.

Crystal, however, was much like a wild horse; there was an unbreakable spirit with strength and courage in her eyes, a trait that many felt needed to be broken. Her father was proud of Crystal. He honored the beauty and grace of his daughter and was often surprised by her maturity.

When Nabi passed on, Crystal was a young woman of fifteen. Once again the captain found himself forced to raise his child alone. Through the years, Nabi had become more than just a nanny to Crystal. She was the mentor and surrogate mother Crystal had needed in her life. While Crystal had the maturity that came with being fifteen, it was an age still needing the guidance and reassurance of a father.

Crystal accompanied her father to his new assignment at Fort Ann, located farther south on a tiny strip of land between two bodies of water. It really wasn't much of a fort anymore, more a group of buildings that served as a depot for the Haul Over Canal, which tied together the Indian River and Mosquito Lagoon area. With the coming "storm from the north," Crystal was about to lose, once again, the most important person in her life. Captain Saunders was to lead the Florida Militia as it joined forces with other Southern states in the greatest war ever fought.

As Captain Saunders prepared to leave for battle, the possibility of not returning made him do something he would have otherwise regretted. He arranged the marriage of his daughter. The captain wanted security for his daughter in his absence, especially with the possibility he might never return.

Finding a suitor for Crystal was not a problem. They lined up for miles at a chance for her hand. The arrangement was finally made with another militia man. A young captain named Wilson Gale was to move out into battle with Captain Saunders. His family was among the original white settlers who had settled the area and harvested the abundant citrus of the region. They also amassed land, influence, and wealth. In a father's eyes, this was the perfect match for his daughter. It gave her refuge and entrance into one of the most influential families in Brevard, if not the entire state of Florida.

Gale, to friends his age, was not known to be a well-mannered young man. He was arrogant, immature, and disrespectful, but like all men, he desired Crystal and wanted to break this wild steed. He wasn't the man Crystal would have chosen as a suitor. In fact, she despised him. The obedience and loyalty Gale showed in service to her father gave her father the mistaken impression that he was a great man and the perfect husband for Crystal. She felt she had no choice but to honor her father's wishes, marry, and consummate her relationship with this man who truly disgusted her. Her only solace: he was to fight in the Great War and *hopefully would not return.*

CHAPTER

14

I spent most of my time on the beach, not doing my usual watching and rating the women as they walked by. My rating system was quite simple, and I prided myself on rating young ladies of legal stature give or take a few years. They were beer rated, a system Craig and I had developed back in high school. Not that we were any type of studs, but hey, it was the guy thing to do. If a girl was hot, we'd say none or one beer. The amount of beer actually suggested how much we would have to drink in order for us to be with the girl or get her in bed. The only exception was if a girl was so hot and out of our league she would get the reverse rating, which indicated how drunk she would have to be to be with us. Even today, I play the game when I'm lying on the beach or hanging out in a bar. It keeps my mind occupied when I'm bored.

Today, however, was different. I was transfixed on the spot on the dunes where the CSI unit was working just the other day and sat facing south, so I could see it better. Even both of the kids saw I wasn't my usual goofy self and asked if I was okay. I told them I was fine and laid my head down on the sand to try and close off my mind and get a little sun.

I dozed into one of those half-in and half-out of sleep modes, rousing myself every so often to check on the kids and the dunes.

At one point, I swear I saw the Indian standing there gazing down at me with his arms extended and eyes looking intently at the ground. Still I could not understand what the meaning of this Indian's presence meant for me, when all of a sudden his gaze became transfixed on me and a feeling of helplessness prevailed. I raised my eyes to his and they locked. I couldn't look away or make a sound. The Indian looked at me and opened his mouth to cry out when a clap of thunder rocked the beach.

"Let's go, Dad," yelled Jessie as she started gathering our gear up. "That was a little too close for comfort." She was right. In Florida we sometimes are a little too brazen. Storms can pop up in an instant and pass as quickly as they arise, but in that instant, they can be deadly. The general rule around the beach is if a thunderhead is east of I-95, which is about six miles away, then the lighting has a good chance of reaching the beach.

As we quickly gathered up our belongings and headed back to the boat, I looked back over my shoulder toward the dune. To my relief, I saw nothing. *I can't believe I was dreaming again.*

The trip back to Honeymoon Lane was uneventful. The ride on the water was a little scary with the continued threat of a storm, but we heard no more thunder. The kids where happy, or at least they seemed to be, probably because they were going home.

We hit the dock, tied up the Whaler, and made it to the Cherokee just as a cloud opened up on us. We placed the wipers on full throttle and drove off.

By the time we pulled into the driveway, the skies had cleared. "Mr. Doctor" was wiping down his Mercedes and turned to wave at me with a smile.

Why not wave and smile, you asshole, you're only banging my ex-wife.

Actually I really didn't care as I once did, but being pissy was sometimes fun. Honestly, he was a really nice guy, and why the two of them were together was beyond me. With his looks, I guess getting the attention of any attractive woman wasn't easy, so Marion was definitely a catch for the good doctor. From Marion's standpoint, prestige and money was definitely the main attraction and not necessarily in that order. Something I promised her but could never give her when we married.

"Hi, Tucker, Marion is in the house. I'll get her for you if you'd like," he called out.

"No thanks, Charles, late for an engagement, but tell her I'll catch up with her later," I yelled. I really had no intentions of catching up with her at all, but it sounded cordial.

I was out of there in a flash. I had no desire to talk with the bitch, and if it were up to me, I wouldn't be catching up with her anytime soon. I ran home to shower and get a fresh set of clothes, and then headed over to Mitch's for my token Saturday night appearance. A few beers and the same old war stories would be fun. A chance to check out half-dressed, drunk, and unhappy wives would also be fun, if not comical. Mitch's wife would be a flirtation target, not that anything would ever come of it, but making the boss's wife feel special was a plus for my working environment. I wasn't planning on staying long. A few hours, and I would be out of there.

CHAPTER

15

As days passed, Osci became a frequent visitor and new worker at the plantation. He returned regularly, not for the provisions or payment the plantation's family provided, but for the chance to see Crystal.

The hope that she might possibly glance his way was enough for him. Even though eye contact and smiles were a norm for her and were frequently exchanged with everyone on a daily basis, she often went out of her way to find Osci at work and make a very special connection with him. Osci believed no one noticed the occasional flirtation, which had become an infatuation for him.

One day he was approached by an elderly Indian worker and was told he was angering the gods and treading in dangerous territory. "No Indian should ever think of a relationship with a white woman," he told him and warned Osci it would never have a chance of succeeding.

Osci was shocked that the old Indian had noticed the growing attraction between him and Crystal. The smiles and starry-eyed glances they gave each other were easy to see. He had let his guard down for the first time in his life, but he didn't care, she was worth it. His feelings for Crystal had grown so strong that he was willing to take a chance. That chance came on a late, hot summer's afternoon.

Osci was making his way along the trail to the water and then to his canoe for the long journey back to his village. The sun was setting and a warm breeze worked its way across the water and rustled the palms. As he approached the river, a sound caught his ear that was not the palms rustling. He came closer to the water and still could not make out where this unexpected sound was coming from.

He made his way through the foliage a short distance to the north and came to a small clearing with beautiful turquoise green water and a sandy beach.

At the edge of the water, lifting herself out from her swim, was Crystal. She was gorgeous to behold. She was totally naked. Osci couldn't move. His eyes were fixed on the beauty of Crystal. Every curve of her body was accentuated by the sun's rays as they glistened off the water. She was absolutely stunning with her large, supple breasts and long, smooth legs. Osci's heart skipped a beat.

As she headed toward her clothing, she paused, as if she could feel his eyes on her. She flipped her head in Osci's direction, and her long, wet hair flew through the air. Osci froze. He wasn't sure if he should run or beg for her forgiveness. He didn't have the nerve to do either.

Crystal smiled; yes, she smiled and stepped in all her beauty toward him. Much like the first time she spotted him, she lifted her hand toward him with a gesture that said clearly, *Come to me.*

The explosion of passion between the two was what they had both believed was meant to be. The softness of Crystal's breasts as Osci cupped them in his hands was beyond anything he had ever felt. Crystal also felt total fulfillment as Osci slipped in between her delicate folds and thrust rhythmically to a beat that only the two of them could hear. They played and explored each other's bodies and souls as they rolled on the sand into the water until darkness blanketed the beach.

Osci and Crystal secretly met regularly as their love blossomed into something neither could deny. For the first time in both their lives they found in each other a comfort that only true love can bring. They knew their love was forbidden and no one could ever know. But the few times they were able to spend together they spent in each other's arms, which for them was enough to make them happy.

CHAPTER

16

I arrived at Mitch's boat, or should I say yacht, about an hour late. Always good to be a little late and make a grand entrance, I was once told. The damn yacht was bigger than my trailer. He once had told me it was purchased in the Mediterranean and sailed—yes, sailed—to Florida. It was a floating mansion with two staterooms, a living area, galley, two full baths, and enough deck space for guests to dance the night away.

Yes, definitely larger than my trailer.

The marina, of course, was one of those state-of-the-art facilities that some Northerner pumped money into after the last hurricane ravaged the area. The place was just off the Eau Gallie Causeway located near a nice area of shops, restaurants, and bars.

The facilities at this place were amazing. It had a pool for all who paid the exorbitant fees. Barbecues were set up at the end of each dock, and there were bathrooms and showers that dockers all had a private key to if they desired not to use their floating homes. There were dining areas, not picnic areas—God forbid you would call them that—under shaded palms. The place was more like a floating condominium complex than a marina.

When I arrived, the party was in full swing. People were all over Mitch's boat—sorry, yacht—and I was greeted by the usual cast of characters whom Mitch invited to all his parties. I went aboard and was greeted by Mitch with a smile and a cold beer.

"Hey, buddy," he yelled over the blaring music. "I've got a cold one right here for my boy."

"Thanks, Mitch. See you got the place jumping. I'm surprised the neighbors haven't complained about the loud music," I shouted over the noise.

"Complain? How can they complain? They're all here," he screamed back at me with a hearty laugh.

My beer was ice cold and felt good on my parched throat. I let Mitch take me by the arm and introduce me to the same people he did at every party.

"Have you ever met my bud Tuck?" he asked everyone we met. No shit! I had probably met most of these people at least ten times before.

In Mitch's defense, there were a few new faces this time. One of the new neighbors was a fellow who just sailed down from New Jersey a few weeks earlier to get away from an ex-wife and the lousy weather. Forgot his name, but he was a hell of a nice enough guy, a bit older than most of the guys there. When I heard *ex-wife* mentioned, I could not help but smile and say, "I feel for ya, fella." We shook hands, laughed, and said we would get together and compare notes some other time.

I got away from him because a discussion about ex-wives was not what I wanted to spend the next hour doing. Mine had caused me enough heartache, so maybe we could talk about it some other time in a quieter place.

Another new face was a guy who worked, I was told, for some group that took care of something or other to do with political elections. Not sure what he actually did, but Mitch said he helped with getting people the votes they needed, whatever that meant. He was kind of a strange dude. He really didn't seem to fit in with everyone else with his suit jacket and tie. Everyone else was dressed in full island-style dress with shorts and flowery shirts and the women with sundresses. I hate politics, so again, not a guy I wanted to talk to. I didn't give him a second thought.

The evening went along better than expected, and I have to admit, one great thing about Mitch's parties was that there were always a lot of beautiful women. Not girls, but established, well-to-do women. The only problem was almost all of them were married to high-profile assholes. Not many were single, and I did at least have a rule I always followed: no married women. Flirting was okay, but nothing more.

The party actually was one of Mitch's better ones, and I had been to most of them. They were usually held at his estate during the holidays, but this was the first one on his new yacht. He spared no expense and always provided the best of everything. Everyone was having a good time and Mitch got me to tell the same old stories he'd heard a million times before to his group of overweight wannabe athletes. Nice guys, with money and trophy wives, but no one I would really consider athletic.

It was good to unwind after a few hectic days and nights, but there was one thing during the evening that made me a little uneasy. Everywhere I turned this new guy with the suit was there within earshot. Not the guy from Jersey with the ex, but the other one who was involved with some type of politics. It seemed I couldn't get away from the guy. Not that we actually had any type of conversation; it was just that he was always within earshot.

I usually recognize the difference between people who want to hang around and slide into one of my conversations because they may have been a player in their day, but this guy was different. I could tell from his expressions he wasn't interested in any of my old sports stories or how I was recruited, made all-state, and had the most promising potential of any athlete in recent memory. He never really spoke to anyone at the party either. I just continued to find it odd that all too often he hung around me.

At one point I even asked Mitch what was up with this guy, and he laughed. Said something along the lines that the guy had just arrived in the area and a friend had asked Mitch to give him an invite so he could network with a few people. Mitch didn't even know the guy that well.

What the heck. I was probably making more out of this than need be. I know I'm in pretty good shape, so maybe this guy played on the other team, as the catch phrase goes. Not that there's anything wrong with that; I always believed to each his own, but it's definitely not for me. I liked the team I was on and the curvy opposition I played against, even though they drove me out of my mind half the time.

It was around one in the morning when the party started to break up. The weather was still great with a light, warm breeze, and the stars sparkled brightly in the night sky. I said my good-byes, gave Mitch's wife a nice hug and kiss on the check, and she responded with a firm squeeze of my ass. I was tempted to respond with the same but decided against it. She was toasted, but damn she was way too hot for Mitch in that tight sundress. Mitch just laughed at her actions and took a slap at my rear but missed, caught his wife on her hip, and almost knocked her overboard. I had to suppress my laughter as she got pissed at Mitch and stamped away.

Everyone exchanged waves as I made my way down the dock to the car for the short trip home. I took my time starting up the Cherokee because I had an eerie feeling I was being watched. I did have a few beers but not a sufficient amount, at least not enough to hallucinate.

As I pulled out of my spot and turned out of the parking lot, I noticed the political guy starting his car up and heading in the same direction. I turned onto the Eau Gallie Causeway so I could jump on U.S. 1 for the ride home. It would be a nice ride with little to no traffic.

After a few minutes on the road, I glanced in my rearview mirror and noticed this guy's car following behind, so I slowed down and let him approach. We made eye contact as he passed, and I waved as he smiled back at me and sped off. *You're overreacting, Tucker,* I said to myself as I yawned. *I really need a good night's sleep.*

CHAPTER

17

I arrived at my humble abode in no time at all. The ride over the river and up U.S. 1 was a pleasure. Windows down, cool breeze blowing through my hair, and Lynyrd Skynyrd's "Free Bird" on the radio. A perfect late night ride for a purebred Florida boy.

There was actually a little nip in the air for late November. So when I got home it felt good to turn off the A/C and open up the windows to the trailer. The change from last week's heat was refreshing.

I was still feeling good from my couple of beers at Mitch's bash, so I turned on the TV, kicked back on the couch, and found an old James Bond movie playing as I drifted off to sleep.

* * *

Tucker found himself isolated, alone in the dark and in the mist that had become a staple in his recent dreams.

He waited for the mist to clear and to catch sight of the Indian, but the Indian he expected to see never came. Tucker could not understand the meaning of this. The Indian was the main character in all his dreams, yet in this one he wasn't present.

As the mist cleared Tucker found himself on the shore. The beach he was on felt so familiar to him. It was the one in his dreams and the location of Ventara's last victim. The same one he was on with the kids earlier that day.

The peculiarity of the dream was not unusual. What was strange was that Tucker was alone. No one was in sight, no sounds of waves, no crashes of thunder and lighting, and other than the reflection of the moon over the calm, clear water and the dune, there was nothing. That too was odd. In all of Tucker's previous dreams there was always a storm. This evening's dream was quiet and calm, yet Tucker felt a need to be on this beach at this moment in time.

A warm breeze blew off the ocean and lifted Tucker off the soft sand, guiding him effortlessly toward a nearby dune. This gave him a feeling of uneasiness, as for some unknown reason he feared the dune, the Indian's dune. Why he feared it, he wasn't exactly sure; it just gave him an uneasy feeling deep in his gut. Tucker had no choice. He drifted over the sea grass and up to the top of the dune he dreaded.

A cloud covered the moon for a moment and darkness encased Tucker. He froze, not knowing what to expect. As the moon made its appearance again and shed light on Tucker, he looked at his feet and saw a bundle. He recognized it at once. It was the Indian's bundle, the one that had been taken from him and flung to the ground.

Tucker froze. He couldn't move. He didn't have to; the bundle beneath him slowly dissolved its cloth layer by layer to reveal itself. Tucker quivered at what he saw. It was the remains of a small child, the Indian's child that had been so brutally slain before the poor man's eyes in one of Tucker's previous dreams.

* * *

Tucker awoke on the couch in his trailer. Unlike the other times, no thunder or lightning woke him, and Tucker was not in a full sweat. He was more composed, probably because he finally understood what the Indian had been trying to show him in his dreams. Tucker, for the first time in a long time, felt tears well up in his eyes. He felt intense, heartbreaking pain and empathy for the Indian and wished he could help. He sat up on the couch and checked the time. Morning was just a short time away, so he sat there with his head in his hands trying to clear his mind.

CHAPTER

18

Sunday I awoke from what I would definitely consider a restless sleep. Sitting down with my cup of coffee, I felt for the first time that the temperature had broken. There was a chill in the air and the floor beneath my feet was cold. Yeah, I know, it's a trailer so it gets colder much faster than a house. The day was certainly cooler than any day this past week, and the slow change from summer to our other season, winter, was starting. My dad always said, "We have two seasons here, summer and winter, nothing in between." That was true, and winter usually meant sixty- to seventy-degree days and forty to fifty degrees at night. Cold enough to dress your youngster in a parka for the early morning bus ride to school.

The dreams I continued to experience had begun to take their toll on me. I no longer believed they were ordinary nightmares. Something was definitely unique about them. The crispness of the dreams, the clarity with which I could visualize them, and the feeling of actually being there was what made them different.

They were all connected, that I understood, but I couldn't figure out what they actually meant. I could remember every one of them and clearly see the star of each episode, the Indian. His facial features, high cheekbones, piercing eyes, and muscular stature were extremely clear, and from what I've been led to understand, that was not supposed to happen in a dream. Sure, you usually knew who the people were in your dreams, but the clarity was never supposed to be that good. The Indian and who he was, as well as what he was doing, was still a mystery to me.

I usually made it a point on Sundays to stop and see Nana. Other than my children, she was my only living relative, and at ninety-three years of age she was as smart and clever as a whip. She was an important figure in my life, and I still enjoyed her company and seeking out her advice. Since I was a child, she and I always had this special bond. With a glance I knew exactly what she was thinking and she was always one step ahead of me as I tried to get away with the usual mischief a youngster will attempt.

I finished my coffee, cleaned myself up for my morning visit, and headed out the door. When I stepped out, the cool air was refreshing. The sunshine was bright and the breeze had a sweetness to it that only came on those crisp, clear days when the temperature starts low and climbs to a comfortable level.

Driving the old Cherokee was actually enjoyable. I threw on my Oakley sunglasses and put the windows down—not out of necessity this time but because it created a comfortable breeze to drive in. No traffic on U.S. 1 also made the morning drive enjoyable for the short trip down to Melbourne and Nana's nursing home.

I arrived around ten and made my way into the bright pink stucco nursing home—or should I say assisted living complex, to be politically correct. It was a quiet complex, just off Riverside Drive in an old section of Melbourne. Nana liked it here because it was nice and quiet and near where she grew up. She was an original Melbourner, born and raised right here in town.

Nana had grown up the only child of a real estate speculator. She never really spoke of her dad, but I believe he must have been tough on her as she grew up, or at least that's what I overhead my dad say once. Any job that consisted of speculating on anything sounded like a chancy occupation at best, even back in the early days of Florida. I'm sure he was as ruthless as the job demanded him to be.

The facility was nice, and each resident had his or her own living quarters. I made my way to room seventeen, knocked, and entered. Nana was at her usual spot, comfortably seated by the window. She was looking at something in the newspaper with a magnifying glass and glanced up at me with a knowing smile that made me realize she was an essential part of my life.

At ninety-three, she was an ageless beauty with grace and confidence. Her long hair, a nice mixture of gray and white, was wound tightly into a bun at the nape of her neck. If it wasn't for the wheelchair she was confined to, I'd swear she could pass for a woman twenty years younger. The only thing I was really scared of was the reality that she could be taken from me at any time.

"Tucker, my love," she said with a smile and a twinkle in her eye.

"Nana, you're looking great on this lovely Sunday morning. You look fantastic. Did you get all gussied up for me?"

I bent over and gave her a kiss on each cheek and she beamed with delight.

"You're such a bullshit artist, Tucker, there has to be a girl out there somewhere you can feed enough of that crap to and hook as a new woman for yourself." She laughed aloud.

One thing about my Nana, she could throw the bullshit with the best of them, and she also had the mouth of a drunken sailor when she was in the mood. She was a hard ass as a young woman and apparently quite the looker whom men chased after in her time. I always told her that I'd bet she was the first real spring break hottie when she was a girl. She'd smile and answer, "Tucker, you're right. I would have won the first wet t-shirt contest too."

You know what, I bet she was right, but that would make her the Spring Break Queen of 1935. Oh wow, that wasn't a thought I wanted stuck in my head.

Old pictures she had of my granddad and herself showed a vibrant-looking woman with short curly blonde hair, a great smile, and a slender figure. Quite a catch for back in the day or, for that matter, any day.

"So Nan, how have they been treating you here? Anyone I need to rough up for ya?"

"Nope, I can take care of myself, Tucker. If there's any roughing up to do, I'll do it. If any of those old perverts try and come onto me, I'll hit them over the head with a frying pan. How's everything going with you?"

"Good, Nan, just the usual, work and hanging out with the kids when I can."

She held her glare on me for a second or two before continuing, "Hmm...the kids good? I hope you see them often. They'll be out of your life before you know it."

"They're great, Nan. Jess is growing up way too fast and into a very lovely young lady who's starting to drive me nuts. As for Carl, he's the stereotypical little boy, always working on some project. All in all they're great kids."

She nodded and glared out her window. "And how about you, Tucker? How are you really doing?"

"Really?" I exaggerated. "I'm actually doing pretty well, not much sleep of late, but I'll get back to normal soon."

"Not much sleep, Tucker?" She looked directly at me. "Is Osci keeping you awake?" she asked with a raised eyebrow. "You know, the Indian in your dreams."

I froze. Did I really hear what she just said? Numbness came over my body. Heaviness filled my chest. I couldn't find the air to fill my lungs. Did she really say *the Indian in my dreams*?

"Nan...Nan, I don't..."

"I know, Tucker, I've always known. Dreams are a mirror to our souls and messages from beyond. They can free our conscience and enlighten us with wisdom and compassion beyond normal beings," she said seriously.

Nana smiled at me and nodded toward the window near her bed where she wanted me to look. That's when I noticed the dream catcher; it had always been there, but I never really paid much attention to it. I was told about it when I was little. I even had one as a small boy, but as usual, I half-listened to the story behind it, but I did remember Nan saying it was an Indian tradition, to hang one near a sleeping child to keep bad dreams away. As the legend goes, only the good or wanted dreams can get through as they enter one's space, and the bad ones were caught in its web to be dissolved at morning's first light. In Nan's opinion, it was good for anyone, not just children. Strange, I know, but right now everything seemed a little bizarre to me.

I was still speechless and had no idea where to go with this or which way it was all headed. This was beyond my comprehension. How could she know?

"Tucker, let's go for a walk. Please push me for a while."

That wasn't a suggestion, it was an order, and I knew the difference. Her whole tone of voice had changed to one I heard only when she wanted to make sure she was taken seriously.

I wheeled Nana out of her room, down the hall, and out the first available exit to the back of the complex. The lawns were immaculately groomed with stately palms, grape leaves, and colorful foliage all indigenous to the area. The concrete walkways weaved in and out of gardens. I chose the one that led down to the river with its short pier.

The sunshine was brilliant, and a gentle, cooling breeze blew between the trees to tantalize the human spirit. We made our way to one of the benches and Nana asked me to stop and sit next to her. I was still in a state of shock and couldn't even think of a thing to say.

"Tucker, my love," she started, "I've known about your dreams for a very long time now. I've watched you grow into the man you are today. We share a special bond—I've always seen you in your dreams as several of our ancestors have seen us. This past week has been no different."

"You watched me have them even as a child? But Nan, I—"

"Listen, Tucker, just listen, and hopefully you'll understand." She went on, "Every soul is an entity to itself and each one has its own levels of accessibility. Yours is of the highest calling and relates directly back to your...our ancestors." She looked straight ahead and went on. "Our family has a long history, and our ancestors' souls are connected to us beyond space and time. The Indian you see, Osci, is one of your great-uncles. I can't recall how many generations back, but it's not many. It seems your uncle Osci has chosen you to communicate with."

"Chosen me? What would he want me for? There isn't a hell of a lot I can do for anyone," I said.

She continued, "What he has selected you for I'm not exactly certain, and that's for you to find out. Now

I want you to listen, because I'm going to tell you again about our family history, as I've tried to educate you so many times before."

I could somewhat remember the stories my grandmother had told me, but as any child would do, I had listened to them as entertainment, not fact, and assumed that although some might be true, she just enjoyed telling me stories.

"I've heard you tell me pieces of our family history before, but I honestly never gave much credibility to them. Oh, I believed some of it and thought we had some pretty cool connections to both the cowboys and Indians, but that's about as far as I thought it went," I mumbled as a headache started coming on.

"Tucker, do you remember why you were given the middle name Lee?"

"Yeah, that story I actually remember. As a kid I thought it was cool that one of my great-great-grandfathers was General Robert E. Lee."

"And do you recall any other part of those family stories?"

"No, not really. I kinda figured as a kid, hell, the South lost the war, so no reason to dredge up the connection, though right now, thinking back, I should have looked into it further."

"Yes, you should have!" She slapped my hand lightly for emphasis. "I'm glad you remember about our bloodline to Robert E. Lee, but now you need to hear about the other side of our family tree, and you need to really listen this time."

She continued, "One of our ancestors married an Indian woman who he met during the Seminole Wars; she was part of the Seminole Tribe. Your great-great-uncle Osci was their son. He's the Indian in your dreams, Tucker. I've thought about this connection for a while, and I myself can't understand why he has chosen you. The only thing I can guess is that his free spirit was similar to yours today. It's important you understand, Tucker. There's a gap in the family tree. When I went back to research this side of the family with your great-grandfather, we found there's no date of death next to Osci's name. I find it so frustrating; I have nothing concrete to tell you about him, just rumors the family has passed down over the years."

"*You* find it frustrating?" I smirked with a half-laugh. "How do you think *I* feel? I have no idea what the hell is happening to me. I thought I was really losing it."

"Tucker, you need to realize you have a direct connection, a bloodline, to the original settlers of Florida, and I'm not talking about the white settlers."

This was certainly becoming interesting, but I wasn't sure what to make of it. If it weren't for Nana knowing of my dreams, I would have blown off everything about souls being contacted and all the mumbo jumbo that goes with it. Now she was starting to make me a believer.

She slapped me again on the arm to refocus my attention. "The Seminoles were the original settlers of Florida and Osci was one of them. As I said, Osci was the free spirit of his tribe and took to doing things on his own, without regard to the traditions or the consequences to his people—very much like you." She patted my hand and gave me a little grin.

"Anyway, no one knows for sure, but as the story goes, Osci got himself involved with a married white woman from a very prominent and powerful Florida family. The husband was away during the Civil War and it seems Osci and this woman fell in love and had a child together. After that, the story stops. There hasn't been any detail to what happened between the two of them or their child in any of the oral or written accounts about our family. But a great-aunt once told me that Osci and this white woman were banished from the area, although there were rumors that something more horrible happened to them."

I just sat there, speechless. From what I'd experienced in my dreams, I was leaning toward the latter—a horrible ending for Osci.

Nana's eyes were glazed, and for the first time in a long time it made me realize how old she really was. She looked tired, and the afternoon sun had shifted across the sky. I looked at my watch and saw that we had sat and talked for over an hour or so. It was definitely time to take Nana back to her room.

Not a word was said as we wound our way back up the path where the nurses were waiting to help Nana get ready for lunch. I gave her a kiss on the cheek, knowing I needed to get out of there and clear my head. "I'll see you soon," I promised.

She smiled up at me with tears in her eyes as I dashed out the door.

CHAPTER

19

I could have done a number of things after leaving Nana's. I could have called Clair, which she expected. I probably should have gone out for a much-needed drink to take my mind off of things. Instead I did the unexpected for me—I headed home with my brain in a fog. I felt exhausted. Not the physical kind of exhaustion I got from shooting hoops, but mental exhaustion, which was much worse. I was brain tired. After the shocking information Nan had thrown at me, I felt like I was back in college cramming for a midterm exam.

The information about my Indian ancestors and Robert E. Lee was something I could research in more detail later; Nana knowing about my dreams had really freaked me out. I still did not understand what was wanted from me. Though the dream sequences were much more lucid, along with what actually happened, I still couldn't get a handle on my involvement in all this.

My dreams had shown me that Osci's infant son had been taken from him and brutally murdered. That was plain and simple to understand, but why it happened was unclear. I also understood from the location of my dreams that the skeleton discovered on Thursday was not Ventara's last victim but that of my Indian ancestor. I guess Osci wanted to make sure his infant son's remains would not be mistaken for someone else's.

Well, at least now the whole thing was a little easier to understand. I could go in to work tomorrow, tell Mitch we'd been barking up the wrong tree with the skeleton story, and when the forensics come back with their results, we could hand it over to the historical society to deal with. As far as my telling everyone the remains were of a long, long distant relative of mine and I saw it all in a dream…*Uh, I think not! I'll keep that to myself.*

Since I had it all organized in my brain, I felt a lot better. Osci should be able to rest in peace once I saw to it that the remains were not be confused for someone else's. That would be my little contribution to my family, and then I would be done with it and able to sleep at night.

Feeling good about myself and my conclusion to all this, I set my sights on a relaxing ride home. Suddenly my cell phone rang "Sweet Home Alabama" as I fumbled through my jeans to locate and answer it.

"Hi, sexy," Clair started as I answered, "miss you."

"Hey, sweet cheeks, how was your weekend without the kids? Good, I hope." Not to be mean, but I really didn't care much how it went since I had enough shit going on for myself, but I thought I'd be nice and ask.

"The time alone was great. A few days without trying to keep teenagers occupied is always relaxing," she chimed.

"Great, sounds good...shit, I think I just ran a light."

She laughed and said, "Oh, no big deal. You know half the cops in the area and the other half were your biggest fans a long time ago...long, long time ago." She was trying to be funny.

"Okay, wise ass," I began, "did you have any troubles with Mr. Ex when you dropped the kids off to him?"

"You mean Daryl? Yeah, he was the usual basket case. He continues to make threats about you and me, but he's harmless as a fly."

Harmless my ass! I wasn't too sure about that. Clair has been divorced for five years and the guy hadn't gone on with his life. She still had a restraining order against him. The guy had a screw loose. He'd chased away three other guys she'd dated in the past, and to be honest, I didn't need any shit from him.

"So, I was thinking," she broke the silence, "would you like to have a little company tonight? It was a lonely weekend without you."

What happened next was a surprise to even me.

I said, "No, not tonight."

I was shocked the second the words flew out of my mouth. I never, ever turned down an evening with a woman—let me rephrase that, a gorgeous woman. I'd also bet my last dollar Clair had never been turned down either.

101

For about fifteen seconds, the phone went silent. "Okay then…is there something going on that I need to know about?"

"No, hon, nothing's the matter, really. I've just had a very long day with Nan and it's burnt me out," I answered with certainty in my voice. I went into some minor details about my and Nan's talk without revealing the meat of our conversation, and I could tell she felt a little better but still unsure.

"So you see, I'm really exhausted and wouldn't be much good to you tonight."

"Is that why you think I want to come over? Tucker, I really thought our relationship had progressed past just sex. I would like to spend time with you and it doesn't always have to end up in bed." The tone of her voice had changed to the one I recognized as the pissed-off version.

Damn, why do women always do this to me?

"I really want to sit and have a long talk with you, I need to get a few things straight in my head," she breathed heavily into the phone.

"I know, I know, I love spending time with you too," I lied. Since I had always thought sex was our relationship, I wondered what other relationship she was envisioning. Guess she wasn't seeing things the same way I was.

I got her off the phone with a few more charming words, but I know she didn't buy it. I didn't think a talk right now would be one that would make us both happy, especially her.

Anyway, I got home in one piece and made my way inside. The temperature outside made for a comfortable evening. Windows were open, I could hear the cicadas, and the dusk of the day starting to set in made for a real peaceful evening.

CHAPTER

20

Tucker drifted through a mist that covered the entire area. This locale was totally different from the other places in his dreams. He didn't have any idea who he was following until the torches in front of him led into the clearing. Lightning and thunder abated and moved away. Tucker saw a larger boat with a number of men in it. He recognized one of them as the man who had swung his sword through the darkness, into the bundle that was taken from the Indian that Tucker now knew to be his uncle Osci. He was also in the boat, but he was seated with his hands tied and his head bowed, never once looking up.

The boat entered an area Tucker felt familiar with, but he couldn't place where he knew it from. He recognized it, but from where?

As Tucker drifted along behind the boat, he noticed the dress of some of the men. They were military—the Civil War era to be exact. After his talk with Nan, this didn't surprise Tucker, but nothing would surprise him now. It at least gave him a point in time to reference.

The boat continued to drift toward the shoreline and, as they approached, he saw that a small breach in the sand allowed water to continue to move inland. They reached a small outcrop in the brush and another boat was already there. The soldiers and their Indian captive climbed from the boat and made their way down a narrow path to a clearing. Tucker noticed additional torches burning as other men awaited their arrival. As Tucker moved closer to the scene in front of him he was astonished at what he saw. There was a woman fastened to a large cypress tree.

Tucker drifted closer to the group and saw the woman was of extraordinary beauty. Chains wrapped around the tree and restrained her. She looked worn and exhausted with parts of her clothing torn off. A number of wounds about her face, shoulders, and body were noticeable. A bullet wound oozed blood from her left arm.

They brought Osci closer to the woman, and their eyes met. Tears began to stream down their faces. The agony in the woman's face could clearly be seen. She had hoped the love of her life had gotten away, and the sight of him without the bundle brought more anguish to her face than any pain the chains and wounds may have caused.

Neither said a word as the Indian was brought to a tree beside her, just out of reach, and chained to it as she was to hers.

Once all the fastenings were checked, the men started to leave. Not a word passed between them. The man who always portrayed authority, the white man who brandished the sword, lingered for a moment, staring at both Osci and

*the woman then spat on them. He spoke quietly for a moment
to both. Tucker could not make out what was said, but was
mesmerized by the scene unfolding in front of him. Neither the
Indian nor the woman acknowledged the captain as he walked
away.*

*As lightening flashed in the distance and thunder rumbled
across the sky, Osci slowly lifted his head and looked directly at
Tucker. Their eyes locked, but unlike before when Osci held his
gaze with blood red eyes, he looked at Tucker now, and he wept.
Tucker realized he was pleading for help.*

Tucker awoke in a sweat.

*This is now really starting to freak me out more so than
before,* he thought to himself. *What the fuck is going on?
Just when I thought I had it all figured out I get hit with
another dream.*

* * *

The clock on the bedside table said 2:20 a.m.

As before, he got up and checked to make sure the
doors were locked, although he was embarrassed to
even admit it to himself.

Tucker had trouble understanding what Osci had
tried to tell him. The whole thing was a lot more involved
than he or Nan could have imagined. Now he had more
to think about and analyze. Who was the woman tied to
the tree?

From what Nan told him she must have been the
woman Osci was involved with. And the Confederate
officer, the last to leave the two, was a person Tucker

needed to find out more about. Obviously he must have been the woman's husband, but who was he?

Tucker got back into bed, but sleep did not come easily. He tossed and turned with a million scenarios going through his mind. Tomorrow would be a very busy day. He needed a lot of questions answered and wasn't really sure where to start. He thought of a number of people he wanted to see. His mind continued to explode with a lot of who, what, where, why, and how. Earlier, everything had seemed to be figured out, tied in a nice, simple package. Now after speaking with Nan and this latest dream, he wasn't really sure what to think.

Tucker only knew that for the first time in a long time a strong sense of family rose in him and that, whether from the past or present, the family had a need to be protected and helped. Tucker lay for a long time just thinking about the experience his great, great uncle had to endure. A list of things continued to grow as Tucker tried to fall asleep. His eyelids finally grew heavier, and sleep snuck up on him.

CHAPTER

21

I originally thought Monday morning would be a good day to tie up loose ends and be done with my so-called investigative reporting. Until last night, I had everything figured out. I planned on marching into Mitch's office and handing him everything tied in a neat little package, but now I wasn't all that sure. Nan had opened my eyes up to the importance of family and the history of our ancestors. No matter how your family is formed, how many people are involved in your life, or how long ago your ancestors may have lived, it is important to keep them alive in your heart and memory. Nan made me realize I am the man I am today from the compilation of all that. Whether good or bad, I owed a piece of myself to my past.

I showered, shaved, and threw on a clean pair of slacks—at least they passed the sniff test—and pulled my old windbreaker from the back of the door to ward off the morning chill as I headed out.

The air was crisp, clean, and made you feel the day would be special. I opened the Cherokee, jumped in, and immediately felt something was wrong. My seat was farther back than usual. Hmm…that seemed strange. I don't think I ever had the seat back this far. My heels didn't even reach the worn-out section of the carpet that took me ten years to imprint. I couldn't remember having any reason to move the seat back. I looked from my new vantage point at all the usual things a driver would see and use, and I realized a few other things were a little out of sync. My sunglasses were out of place, and the usual clutter on the floor was scattered about. Not much, but enough for me to notice.

Oh well, as I said before, there was nothing to steal here in old reliable. So I shook it off and headed for the office, all the while laughing to myself at the thought of some idiot having actually tried to steal my car. I wondered how long it took him to realize it was worth… well…about nothing.

U.S. 1 was busy as usual with commuters heading north to Cocoa and south to Melbourne. I pulled into my usual Quick Mart for my morning coffee and donut…okay, two donuts. I turned my head to the news stand and almost fainted at the headlines I saw in the Orlando newspaper.

Child Killer Ventara Commits Suicide

I grabbed the newspaper and read further.

Staff Reporter:
Convicted child killer Eddie Ventara took his own life last night, committing suicide in his cell at Raiford State Prison. Guards on their late evening rounds found Ventara at 1 a.m. this morning hanging by cloth shredded from his shirt.

Mr. Ventara is better known as the Central Florida child serial killer, convicted for a string of murders committed over the past five years. Ventara's last victim's remains were reportedly found last week, beachside, buried in a shallow grave beneath a sand dune.

Mr. Ventara was on death row awaiting execution.

Bullshit! No fucking way that man took his own life. He gave me no indication last week he had any intention of committing suicide. In fact, it was quite the opposite. He had appeared impressed with his past events. Why would he kill himself? The asshole was to be executed within the next three months and could have played the whole thing out in front of the media, right up to the end. No way had he taken his own life, not now. It made no sense.

My cell phone rang and Mitch was on the line.

"Tucker, where the hell are you? Did you see—"

I cut him off before he could say another word. "I just saw it, Mitch, and I'm as shocked as you are."

Mitch sounded agitated. "How the hell did you miss this one?"

"I'll be there in ten minutes. This whole thing is too strange."

I hit the pedal hard and made it to the office in seven minutes flat. I was on the pavement running even before the car was parked and shut off.

Running into the office and down the hallway, I was so preoccupied with the news I blew off the customary good mornings and usual chitchat. People looked at me in surprise as I ran past, considering it wasn't the Super Bowl or March Madness time of year. Clair turned to talk to me, but I was past her before the first few syllables left her lips.

I flew into Mitch's office and he immediately said, "Tucker, how the hell did we not hear of this one? I'm not blaming you; since that bitch of an old girlfriend of mine didn't even have the decency to give me a call."

"Well, Mitch, I guess she figured you're all out of favors." I smiled and immediately realized it was the wrong time to try and crack a joke, but shit, it was a habit. Mitch just looked at me.

I jumped back in, "Mitch, there's no way this guy offed himself; he was so pompous and cocky when I spoke to him on Friday."

"Okay," Mitch said. "Let's see how we can salvage some of this. At least you were the last reporter to spend some quality time with him," he smirked.

"Hold on here," I said with a grimace. "That's not funny."

Mitch went on, "And we can use that angle in our article. All the other news agencies will have the same BS, but at least you can quote him with some of his last words… right?" He looked at me hard with the question lingering in the air. "You can quote him, can't you, Tucker?"

"Of course I can," I said. "But Mitch, the beachside remains weren't—"

Mitch cut me off. "Okay now," he said as he got up and started to pace the office. "We can go with the usual crap everyone always jumps on board with, plug in the info about his last victim being found, and use a few quotes from his last interview with you."

"Mitch!" I shouted. "That's just what I've been trying to tell you—his best quote was his last, the one where he looked straight at me and said the remains on the dune were not his victim's."

Mitch still paced in deep thought.

"Mitch!" I shouted. "Did you hear me? The remains are not his last victim's!"

Mitch turned. "What are you saying, Tucker, are you bullshitting me? Did you really go see this guy? 'Cause I have a fax from the coroner's office this morning with a cover letter from the sheriff's CSI unit stating the DNA matches the poor family of his last victim. As a cold case, they've kept it all on file."

DNA was kept on file for this case because the single mother of the child Ventara murdered had moved away shortly after the child was officially recorded as a murder victim. She later committed suicide. Ventara hadn't just murdered the children; his actions had far reaching effects that ripped at the hearts of many.

Mitch picked up the faxes from his desk and waved them at me. My head started to spin. I was shocked by his words.

Sheriff's office? Couldn't be! Not after everything I'd experienced. Why would anyone say it was his last victim? I had the words from Ventara's mouth, what my dreams showed, and what Nan told me. I didn't get any of this.

"Tucker…Tucker, do you hear me?" Mitch yelled.

My attention was back, but it took me a second to hear his words. "Mitch, I swear to you everything is true."

Just then the phone rang, Mitch answered, and in a second his voice was back to its usual sweet self. I just sat there staring, my mind so confused. The circuits in my brain were not connecting and I couldn't think straight.

Mitch returned from his call and sat quietly behind his desk.

"Okay, that was Debra…Lieutenant Nicholson… from Raiford Prison. I put a call in to her this morning when I heard the news because I was surprised I didn't hear it from her first. Not that I'm questioning you, but she just confirmed you were there and apologized for not giving me the heads-up on Ventara. Turns out she had a rare weekend off camping with her new boyfriend. Lucky bastard, the guy must have had the time of his life banging the shit out of her," Mitch said.

Now that I couldn't disagree with. Yep, somebody was a lucky son of a bitch.

Mitch went on, "Anyway, she didn't get any of the information until she arrived at her desk this morning."

We both sat staring at each of other not knowing what to say.

I finally spoke first and calmly said, "Mitch, the guy said it was not his last victim and I believe him. Something really strange is going on here. I can't put my hands on it, but give me time to find out. You asked me to do a bang-up job for you—and I will if you let me. Give me a chance and I'll do some real investigative reporting for you."

He smiled and thought for a second. "Okay, Tucker. You say something doesn't seem right here, and I agree with you. I guess a day or two at most won't hurt, we do have the last interview angle to run with him...don't we, Tucker?"

I smiled back and hesitated for effect. "You bet your ass we do, buddy, just give me forty-eight hours and I'll have it all in black and white for you and ready to print."

Again he smiled. "Well, what are you waiting for? The clock is ticking, get the hell out of here."

CHAPTER

22

I walked out of Mitch's office in a fog. I was eager to get started, but I was totally shocked by this change in events and really had a hard time getting my bearings. I know people say I may not be the brightest banana in the bunch, but damn, it wasn't out of the realm of reason I shouldn't have a hard time putting things into perspective.

I had a number of questions on my mind, and I knew exactly who I should contact. Actually, there were a few people I had in mind, and the first one was Craig, my buddy from the Brevard County Sheriff's Office. I planned on calling him as soon as I got back to my office...okay, cubicle.

On the way there I was intercepted and side-tracked for a good twenty minutes. It was Clair, and she was on me like...like, well, you know the phrase. She grabbed me and pulled me into the coffee lounge and demanded we have a talk and that we talk NOW.

Now, I'm not a bad guy, but when someone demands something I don't think they need at the time, well, let's just say I don't handle it well and start making my own demands. My ex started demanding a lot from me, and I demanded the exit route from the relationship.

"We need to talk," Clair hissed.

"Not now, Clair. There are a lot of things going on, and I need some space to handle it."

"You need space?" she screamed. "After all this time and quality evenings we had together, you tell me now you need space right out of the blue! Was I just another lay for you? You can come up with a better excuse than that to dump me!"

She was right, I could come up with a million excuses, I was good at that, but she had it all wrong. I wasn't trying to dump her, but put me under enough pressure and anything could happen.

"No, I'm not asking for that kind of space, and you're not just another lay. Actually you're a fantastic lay." Again, not funny and really bad timing. I spoke carefully, not to say something I might regret later. Nah...I knew myself, I wouldn't regret it later.

"Clair, listen," I began. "There's something strange going on with the project Mitch gave me. I need some space to get all my thoughts together and finish the job."

She looked at me strangely with her head tilted to one side. "You're trying to tell me you're on some special project that's not sports related? I find that hard to believe," she said with a laugh.

"Well, believe it," I said. My temper was growing short. Was she mocking me as a reporter? I know people took me lightly at times because of my carefree exterior, but when things needed to get done, I was your man. Just give me the ball with the clock ticking down and get out of my way. I was the guy who would finish the game off.

Be careful what you say, I reminded myself. One thing I learned over the years was if she—or any woman, for that matter—pushed our relationship and played tough, I could and would do the same. I could be a stubborn SOB, and that related right back to my playing days. There's a lot of fish in the sea, as they say, and most of them were partially dressed here in paradise.

I continued, "I'll fill you in on everything when I get the time, I promise." I actually kept my composure and started to walk away.

"Well, get the time soon," she sneered, "'cause the clock is ticking. You know I could easily divert my gracious intentions in another direction." Her voice slowly faded into the air as I walked away.

That's just great, another deadline, and one I didn't want to deal with at this moment. But I was happy that I had actually kept my composure as I finally got back to my cubicle and sat to look for Craig's cell phone number. Rummaging through my desk, I noticed my message light flashing on my office phone.

Beep...first message: "Tucker, it's me. You haven't answered your cell, so I'm calling you at your place of work...yeah, work, that's a funny one. I still haven't received your child support check, and my patience has run out. Do I really have to do this every freaking month? You're such an—"

Delete.

I really didn't need to hear any shit from her, now or ever.

Beep…second message: "Hi, Tucker, this is Craig. I need to talk to you, but not over the phone. Give me a call ASAP and we'll set something up."

Great, he beat me to the punch on this one. I immediately dialed the number Craig left, and he picked up on the second ring.

"Tucker, it is Tucker, isn't it?" he exclaimed.

"Yeah, Craig, it's me," I said as we skipped the pleasantries. "What do you have for me? Because I certainly have a few questions for you. A lot of strange shit is going on around here."

He answered quietly, "Tucker, there's a lot of weird shit going on around here as well. I can't put my finger on it, but I'll fill you in like I promised I would over on the beach the other day, but not over the phone."

I was taken aback. What did that comment mean? Not talk over the phone? Did he really think our phones could be bugged? Why us, and for what reason?

All this shit couldn't be over a one hundred and forty-plus-year-old skeleton everyone mistook for some psycho's victim! Could it be that simple? I had much of my thoughts and ideas in pretty good order, but maybe, just maybe, there was more to this whole mess than met the eye.

"Craig, I agree, so let's meet at our usual watering hole. Say around tourist time; we can talk things over," I suggested.

"Okay, sounds good." He actually laughed. "I'll see you at tourist time," he said and hung up.

Actually I was pretty damn proud of myself. I was able to camouflage our meeting place and time, just like Bond...James Bond would have done in any of his classic movies. Our meeting place was P.J.'s, known to us as the Watering Hole, as I so cleverly disguised it. And "tourist time" was a running joke between the two of us; it meant five o'clock, taken from Alan Jackson and Jimmy Buffet's song, "It's Five O'clock Somewhere." We both loved the song, so the simple use of the song's title became a natural when ever we spoke about meeting up and having a few beers.

Hey, this investigative thing wasn't so bad. I was set with Craig, and now I needed to make a stop to see one more person who could help me try and make some sense out of all this before I met with Craig. I grabbed my keys, made sure I had my cell phone, and I darted out of the office before anyone else could accost me, especially Clair and any counterattack she might launch on me with more questions about our relationship. I wasn't in the mood to hear any more from her. As much as I liked Clair, now was not the time to deal with our personal life.

CHAPTER

23

I made it to the faithful Jeep with out any distractions. The weather was still great and a gentle warm breeze floated through the windows. I fired her up, hit U.S. 1, and made the turn before the light turned red. I knew exactly where I wanted to stop first before I met Craig— the Melbourne library.

I was never a great student; not horrible, but not great. I did have a few teachers I thought were inspiring, but sports were more my thing, and actually, if it weren't for interscholastic sports, I probably would have quit school and tried my hand at professional surfing.

It's a shame with school budgets being slashed that sports are always on the chopping block first. Politicians, who know little about the classroom, always think a majority of kids are there for an education with athletics and the arts on the side. If they only understood that athletics and the arts are the reason some kids are there. Oh well, that's a fight for another time.

I did have a number of fantastic teachers and coaches in my life. Coach Elderly's wife, Cyndi, was one of them. She, along with Coach, took me under their wing when my dad passed. His death took me a long time to get over, and while he schooled me on the court, Mrs. C was relentless on me in the classroom. Nan made sure she was always there for moral support and to keep me grounded, but Mrs. C was my English teacher and the real reason I selected journalism as my major in college. Being the usual kid having troubles getting what was in my head out on paper, Mrs. C always made the transition easy for me. She also opened my eyes to literature, which was a little unusual for a jock like me.

Mrs. C was a gem. She retired a few years back and, after a few months of retirement, couldn't relax. She then decided to take a job for the county in the library system. Perfect fit for the library and a woman who loved to read and write. She even started a program called "Reading for Coins," a system where kids received plastic coins as credit for books they read and later exchanged them for toys and trinkets. A month after she started the program, attendance from young children increased by over one hundred percent. The paper even did a story on her, and the interest in the program continued to grow. The library did a great job offering every age in the community something of interest.

After a short ride I got to the library on Riverfront Drive and was surprised to see how crowded it was for a Monday. I found a primo spot under an old palm, jumped out, and quickly walked toward the door. The puffy clouds and blue sky of November accentuated the beauty of a prime piece of real estate on the river. One thing was unusual: I had a feeling again of being watched. Not the first time I had it, but definitely strange. Oh, what the hell, just my overactive imagination again, I thought. I did secretly hope if someone was watching, it was a five-foot-seven-inch blue-eyed blonde, preferably a divorcee with no baggage.

Aaah, I crack myself up sometimes.

Approaching the desk, I waited for an available clerk and asked if Mrs. C was in and if so, where I could find her. The woman replied that she was and pointed me in the direction of the children's section. I spotted her with a small group of preschoolers, their eyes as wide as saucers as she read aloud to them.

She spotted me and a large grin formed across her face as she signaled me with her finger…one minute. It really took fifteen minutes for her to finish, but I actually enjoyed listening as it took me back a few years… okay, a lot of years.

When she finished she came over and gave me a long hug. "It's been a while, Tucker," she said and smiled. "You have to stop by and visit more often."

"That's why I'm here. I wanted to see you reading to the little ones. Kind of brought back old memories," I smirked.

She took me by the arm, and we strolled into the open area of the library.

"See me read?" She laughed. "More like you're here checking out the single moms."

Yea, she knows me all too well.

I grinned. "Mrs. C, I did stop to see you in hopes you could help with some info."

"Oh really," she said. "That can be arranged as long as you promise to stop over for dinner with Coach and me one night."

Deal," I jumped at the offer.

"Okay, Tucker, what do you have in mind?"

I filled her in on the Ventara case and the skeletal find that was in the news and told her things just didn't add up. I didn't bring up my dreams; I wanted her to take me seriously, and I thought it might creep her out. I asked for a little help researching some history of the area from about one hundred and forty years ago.

"So you're doing some investigative reporting now? That's fantastic!" She smiled. "And you believe the skeleton is from the past and not one of Ventara's victims?" she questioned. "Is that what you're saying?"

"Exactly, I need to look back as far as possible and see if there are any stories about unsolved disappearances involving adults and infants."

She looked at me funny as she stopped in her tracks and asked, "Adults? Why would you think that? I don't recall reading anything in the newspaper about an adult skeleton being found. I thought a child's remains were getting all the attention. Where did you get that information?"

I didn't answer, just had a look on my face that showed I didn't want to answer. Kind of like the cat caught with the canary in its mouth.

"Okay," she said and frowned. "You don't have to answer. Good journalists never reveal their sources...at least not until they're threatened with jail."

Yeah right, my source was a dream, a ninety-three-year-old lady, at least for now, and hopefully a sheriff's officer in a few hours. I doubted that would go over real well in the world of journalism. They'd have me writing comic strips after that one. That's why I needed to look back and find some concrete info.

"Let's see," she said as she led me to the research area. "We have a lot of maps of the area starting back when the county was settled. They're actually pretty accurate. They show the land parcels as they were divided among families and later into towns.

"Over here," she went on, "is our computer system. You can log on and pull up as much history as you want. Can I help you find anything in particular?"

"You know, I'm not really sure what I'm looking for yet, but I'll know it when I see it."

She smiled and checked the time. "I have a hectic schedule the rest of the day, but if you need help, ask for Carol at the front desk. She's single too. She'll be glad to help you, and next time don't be a stranger for so long. We miss you."

She gave me a peck on the cheek and left me to my research.

Time flew by, and before I realized it, three hours had passed. I spent all the time looking through the computer system at anything dating back to the Civil War and what would now be Brevard County. I checked everything from the Historical Society to records the state kept on file. I found nothing substantial except a lot of interesting tidbits about the area and the various families that settled here. The names I kept in the back of my mind for reference. But nothing actually caught my eye.

I took a ten-minute break to stretch my legs and well...well, check out Carol. By my first look it was obvious she wasn't my type. Oh well.

After rubbing my eyes and stepping over to the atlases, I decided to start searching old maps of the beach where the infant skeleton was found. Nothing of importance was noted on any of the maps; the beach area hadn't even been named. So thinking back to my dreams, I scanned the map back across the water toward the mainland and the direction I believed Osci must have traveled. It was then I realized Merritt Island was actually the first piece of land someone would run into following Osci's route in my dreams. There was no way a canoe could have paddled from the mainland around Merritt Island trying to avoid capture. It was just too long a journey, even by today's standards. Osci must have started his ill-fated trip from somewhere in the Merritt Island area.

I closed one map book, checked the time, saw I had about another thirty minutes before I needed to leave, and looked through another large atlas. I finally found one with a section dedicated to the settlement and development of Merritt Island. Flipping through a few pages I came across a map showing what I figured must have been Osci's starting point for his trip across the river to the beach.

I was unfamiliar with the origin or history of the area, but I did remember Merritt Island had consisted of a number of small ranches and citrus plantations that were eventually combined into one. I now looked a little more carefully at the map and something strange caught my attention.

One area of the island had a name next to it that, according to the pronunciation, sounded like one I recognized. Though the spelling was different, the pronunciation was one I had heard before.

Could it be a coincidence?

No, it couldn't be!

A light bulb seemed to explode in my head as I looked at the name.

Son of a bitch. It has to be. Mother f…

This was way too strange.

It never dawned on me that a connection might lie closer to me than I realized. How could this be? The name was very well known, and the longer and deeper I became involved in this story, the weirder it continued to become.

Damn, at least now I had a name from the map that I was all too familiar with and could actually look into. The more I thought about it, the less shocking the name became. Shit, I thought to myself, but what would that name have to do with Osci? I needed to find out. It could all end up being nothing, but it was a stone I couldn't leave unturned.

I closed up shop, grabbed my windbreaker, and with a name in my mind—whether right or wrong—headed out to meet Craig.

I was getting into my car when the hair on the back of my neck stood up. A strange feeling of being watched once again came over me. Now this was happening way too often for my liking. I turned around and walked to the back of the Cherokee acting as if I was looking for something when I spotted a car pulling away. I'd seen it before, but where?

CHAPTER

24

With the switch to standard time a few weeks ago, you could definitely feel the change of seasons coming. The sky lost its brightness a little earlier, and shadows from the palms stretched farther each day. This afternoon, the air was cool and a light drizzle fell from scattered clouds. Though the weather report was calling for the return of one more warm front by the end of the week, in truth I welcomed the relief from this past summer's excessive heat. I do love the warm weather, but the little cold snaps we have on the Space Coast are always a welcome and pleasant change—unless of course they last too long.

I slowly glanced around as I pulled out onto Riverfront. I looked right, left, and deliberately held my glance a little longer to the right. There again, that all too familiar car sat along the shoulder of the roadway, just waiting.

The drive up to Cocoa Beach to meet Craig wasn't long. I jumped on the Eau Gallie Causeway and worked my way up A1A past Satellite Beach and Patrick Air Force Base. Though this was a short ride north, with Patrick on the left and the emerald Atlantic on the right, it was one of the nicest drives along the coastal highway.

I arrived at P.J.'s a bit later than our agreed time, around 5:20, and immediately made my way into the bar. The place had a nice little crowd for a Monday night. Fred made eye contact with me, we shared a wink, and he quickly handed me my favorite beer, as any good bartender would. With a flip of his head he directed me to the back corner of the room where Craig was waiting.

"Gotta love that service," I proclaimed with a huge grin as I approached Craig.

"Don't be so surprised. I told him you were coming and to have the Land Shark waiting," he shot back with a smirk.

Craig was in plain clothes, seated at a small booth, his back to the wall as he quietly rotated his beer mug between his hands. He gave me a smile, nodded for me to sit, and pushed a bowl of pretzels my way. His real attention was on the entrance as he appeared to scan every person who walked through the door. It kind of reminded me of our younger days, but this time he wasn't looking to check out a prospective female companion for the evening as we used to; his stare was a little more serious.

"Eaten yet?" he asked.

"No. Why, you hungry?" I responded and immediately remembered that as I had hurried around all day I forgot to have lunch, not even a snack, which was so unlike me. I was so caught up in my research and running things through my mind I must have totally blocked out the hunger pains that hadn't developed until now.

We called a waitress over and ordered sandwiches to munch on as we settled into our second round of drinks.

"So, old friend, what have you been up to?" I said sarcastically.

"What have I been up to? The question is what the fuck have you been up to?"

He asked in such a way that I suddenly realized this whole Ventara thing might be a little more involved than either of us originally believed. I thought for a second and chose my words carefully.

"Well, let's see," I continued. "I've actually been working. My editor has been on my back to complete a story about the skeleton you guys found on the beachside last week."

"Go on," Craig said with interest in his voice.

I wasn't happy being the one doing all the talking; it almost felt as if Craig was interrogating me. What was I, back in high school? Explaining my plans to my date's father for after the prom?

Yes, sir, with all due respect, after the dinner and dancing, I plan on getting your daughter drunk, her bra and panties off, and banging the shit out of her on the beach. Oh yeah, the things I could have said if I could do it all over again. The thought actually made me smile for a second.

I snapped out of it, and figuring Craig had reasons he'd eventually share with me, I continued, "Since then I've visited the federal prison, spoke to Ventara and—"

"Wait, you what?" he stopped me in mid-sentence. "You spoke to that little piece of shit? Didn't he just commit suicide?"

Craig was one of the lead investigators on the missing children cases and the arresting officer of Ventara five years earlier, so his feelings were easily understood. You don't work on cases like Craig does and see what he does on a daily basis without it affecting you in some way or other. I can remember him telling me why so many officers became divorced alcoholics. It's this type of fucked-up case that can cause a man to hit the bottle and just say fuck it all.

It's so depressing dealing with brutal crimes, especially those involving kids. Later on everyone expects the investigators to go about their normal lives and leave work at the workplace. It just doesn't happen.

"Well, what's strange is," I said with a sip of beer, "I spoke with him a day before his suicide, and Craig, there's no way he was planning to end it all."

Craig just listened with no expression on his face. His eyes never changed, but he nodded his head for me to continue.

"He also told me the remains everyone is giving him credit for are not his."

There was silence for half a minute as our waitress approached and delivered two more fresh beers. "Fred said to keep you happy with one in the hand." She smiled and quickly retreated.

"Tucker," Craig said, regaining my attention, "what exactly did Ventara say to you?"

"Well, I can't remember exactly, but he said the remains were not his. He was adamant the last victim would never be found or disturbed. He said it was to rest in peace, and Craig, I believed him. Now I'm told this morning by my boss that the sheriff's office said the remains *are* his last victim's. What the hell is going on here, Craig?"

I knew my question got a reaction from Craig as I saw his eyes widen. We both were quiet for a bit longer as we took a few sips of our beer and ate our sandwiches, a nice distraction to let everything sink in.

A minute or two later Craig finally spoke. "Tucker, you said some weird stuff was going on. I really don't want to agree, but I'm starting to feel the same way."

Now my eyes went wide and my ears perked up. I was anxious to hear what he had on his mind.

Craig started, "Tuck, this stays between us for the time being. No journalism shit now, agreed?"

I shook my head in conformity.

He continued, "I never gave much support to it, but what you just said were the exact same words Ventara said to me five years ago when I nailed the asshole. I never gave it much credence and figured the piece of shit was talking out his ass, but hearing you say the same thing just made the hairs on the back of my neck stand on end."

Mine too, I thought.

He went on, "Last week I thought we'd finally tied up the last loose end of a cold case that's haunted me—and the entire area—for years. At the beach site I actually felt we had some closure, but now I'm not sure. I was feeling good about everything when I saw you, but everything changed this morning."

"Go on," I said. "You've got my full attention." Now I felt like the interrogator. I took another drink—or should I say chug. I was starting to feel as if I needed a lot to drink while the information was being shared.

"I got the coroner's report this morning and it read what I knew it *shouldn't*—that it was Ventara's victim."

I put up my hand to stop his talking. "Hold on a second, you're saying you believed the findings would show it wasn't his? Why?"

"Last week back on the beach, the on-the-scene CSI unit explained to me, after you left, what they believed was the cause of death according to the condition of the skeleton. They're pretty good predicting the cause of death during their initial investigation. I have no reason to doubt them, but I double checked Friday night with a friend of mine in the coroner's office."

I was intrigued by this information and was now hanging on to Craig's every word. I adjusted my seat and waited for him to continue.

"The CIU guy at the beach the other day told me the cause of death was decapitation, without any hesitation and with 99.9 percent accuracy. The head and much of the upper torso was detached from the rest of the skeleton. Some type of sharp object, much like a sword or machete, struck the victim with enormous force a number of times. As you know, this wasn't Ventara's method."

Craig was right. I knew and cut him off by saying, "Suffocation was his method." I also had a pretty good idea from my dreams what type of weapon was used on this poor child as well as knowing who the victim's father and mother were.

Craig looked at me and smiled, but it was not one of those happy smiles. He looked tired.

"What about the coroner? Did they confirm this?" I whispered.

"I personally went over and spoke with Karla Santiago," Craig continued.

Karla was one of Craig's flings. I had met her a few times at different social events and thought she was an absolute Latin beauty. I never hit on her because of my closeness to Craig. Don't get me wrong, I would have loved to, but because she was a girlfriend of Craig's, I wouldn't cross that line. We did playfully flirt with one another, but she knew of our close friendship and played it off as fun.

She was a smart, important piece of the sheriff's CIS unit and had become one of the leading experts in her field. She usually got the call to testify as the expert witness when things went to trial. That's where the two of them met, at the Ventara trial. Though the relationship had cooled off, they remained close friends and could trust each other for information when needed.

"She confirmed the remains were exactly what the initial recovery showed, plus the state of the skeleton indicated it was not a fresh find," Craig whispered as he took another sip. "It was a lot older than you or me."

All this did not surprise me as it probably should have. I had my own beliefs about the remains and now truly believed Osci was communicating with me about his child. My God, he actually witnessed his child's murder!

I started back. "So why would Karla submit a fake report?"

"That's just it," said Craig. "She didn't. She was overridden by her superior and told she messed up a few important pieces of evidence. He said he'd take the case off her hands and do the report himself. You know how good she is, Tuck. She doesn't make mistakes like that."

Craig glanced over the restaurant and lost his concentration for a moment.

"What is it?" I said with concern, now looking over my shoulder.

"Nothing," he went on, "just felt like someone was staring in our direction."

Now the hairs were standing up on the back of my neck in addition to goose bumps on my arms.

"Anyway," he said, "where was I? Oh yeah, Karla is the best at what she does, and she doesn't make mistakes like her boss was suggesting. She's meticulous almost to a fault. And what bothers me more is when I questioned my own superior about the report, I was told to mind my own business and the case was closed."

I could tell Craig was bothered by all this. He was a good friend I'd known for a very long time, and though he had his own issues as we all do, he was the ultimate professional when it came to his job.

"What do you make of it? Does any of this make any sense to you?" I asked.

"That's just it, Tuck. In my line of work I'm trained to question things and look through the forest for each tree. None of this makes sense and I smell a...I hesitate to say it...a cover up. Covering what? I don't know, it doesn't make sense, but it has to be something big and important to someone."

I agreed. Something wasn't right. For a second I considered telling him about my dreams, and finally thought, what the hell, if you can't trust a friend, who can you trust? So I decided to give him a short synopsis.

Craig already knew a bit of my family history; he never left my side at my dad's memorial, so I told him a little more about the family, what Nan said, and the dreams I had. I knew some of this wouldn't be a total surprise for him.

I couldn't read him, but he listened intently. Whether he thought I was crazy or not, he didn't stop or question me.

When I finished, he finally spoke. "You know, Tuck, I've heard a lot of strange stuff, but what makes your crazy story make sense is that it holds water and fits more than anything else I've got."

I smiled with a bit of relief. Other than Nan knowing about my dreams, Craig was the first person I had really told, and it felt like a load off my shoulders.

He finished, "And being an investigator, I wouldn't discount anything you say, even if it's from a dream. Some investigators rely a lot on supernatural things, like those who use psychics. I personally wouldn't go that far, but I certainly don't think you're crazy."

We sat in silence sipping our beers for a good ten minutes, both lost in our thoughts. We agreed to get back in contact with each other tomorrow, no matter what, and compare our findings. Both of us planned on doing our own research, so a comparison of our notes was a good idea.

We paid our bill, gave our gratitude to Fred, and stepped outside into the chill of the evening air. It was now nine thirty and the cold front had passed and clearing skies were now evident. We shook hands and headed in different directions.

CHAPTER

25

So much information was swirling around in my head that it gave me a headache you wouldn't believe. I hadn't felt this way since pulling all night cramming sessions in college during exams. At least back then, with the snap of my fingers, I could easily find a co-ed to soothe my pain.

Ah, the memories. They brought an immediate smile to my face. They also made me wonder what Clair was up to tonight. That thought brought on laughter. After our encounter, I was sure she'd want to be as close to me right now as she would to a cattle prod.

Leaving P.J.'s, I made a decision to ride around a little to clear my thoughts before heading to my humble abode. I decided to zip over the causeway and hit South Tropical Trail. Taking it south, along what at one time had been Osci's hunting grounds and the location of a few large plantations, gave me some insight into what it must have been like so long ago. I never really looked at this area in such a light.

The temperature had dropped off, and the air flowing through my open windows actually gave me a chill. As a true Floridian, I refused to roll up my windows and wouldn't, even if it got a little colder. I could admit, with no hesitation, when it was warm and even when it was hotter than hell, but I would never admit it was ever too cold here in paradise. This was certainly an enjoyable November evening; at least I told myself that to make the night's events easier to swallow. I did cheat a little by putting the floor heat on to keep my feet warm, but that was a little Southern secret I would never tell.

The drive along the trail is always gorgeous. Homes are immaculate with their manicured lawns and gated driveways. In the evening, palms are lit up with colored lights. It's all really pretty, and tonight was no exception. Many of the more expensive homes—okay, mini-mansions, since they have a price tag in the millions—have fantastic views of the Indian Lagoon and Banana River.

My children live in one of these homes with my ex and the good doctor. They actually have one of the nicer places in the Honeymoon Lake area. A quiet, picturesque piece of land with many spots still undeveloped by man.

Ah, the life. It must be nice. That was the only thing I felt good about in our divorce—at least now the kids were living a lifestyle I never could have given them and the good doctor could. He actually wasn't such a bad guy. On the other hand, the ex…well, she was still an asshole.

As I passed their street, I gave a wave for the kids and the middle finger salute for my ex.

Continuing my drive, I tried to visualize what the area must have looked like during Osci's time. One single dirt road most likely cleared the way to the plantations, and boat traffic probably provided the primary means of transportation. Fruit trees spread in all directions, and everything from oranges, grapefruit, pineapples, coconuts, and mangos to bananas were part of the crop that a plantation might grow and harvest. As time passed a few of these fell out of favor, but oranges, grapefruit, and mangos were still a big product harvested in the area. There were actually still a few small groves, with fences around them, in between the beautiful homes. From what I understood, a lot of home owners tried to get tax write-offs by claiming they still farmed. Yeah okay, if you believe that, I have a causeway I would love to sell you!

I could also see today's mini-plantation owners driving their Escalade pickups in white tuxedos and hats as they collect their fruit. That would actually be a funny sight.

The only negative along this path was the large number of for sale signs that sat on the edge of all the small orchards. Their presence suggested that these small pieces of tax deduction would eventually be plowed under to construct someone else's mini-mansion.

I drove farther south and made a left onto the Pineda Causeway and found a spot to pull over. From my vantage point to the left, I could see the flickering lights of the Tropical Trail homes upriver. To the right, Patrick Air Force Base lit up everything as far as the eye could see. Just another of Uncle Sam's prime pieces of real estate.

Trying hard, I could almost envision Osci paddling along in his canoe, heading over to the beach, being followed by a number of larger boats with their torches lighting the sky. It would have to be a very simple course for the Indian to follow from what I saw on the library map. Yet the cover of night would conceal many landmarks needed in his escape. It would also have to be a very short distance to travel for the pursuers as they chased Osci in their larger, more powerful boats. I stood for a number of minutes and just stared.

I broke the stare as the roar of a large transport came in to land at the base. As I looked around it made me realize why I loved this area of Florida so much. Sometimes I take it for granted, but the Space Coast area is one of the little secrets that still exist in this state of Mickey Mouse. The population had grown as people discovered its beauty, but it could have been worse—at least the county seemed to have learned from others' mistakes and taken the time to plan and map things out for future growth.

I smiled; my headache had subsided, so I took a deep breath of crisp, cool air and decided to head home.

Feeling good with my headache all but gone, I cranked the radio up, set my course to U.S. 1 and my "trailer park community." It wasn't like Tropical Trail, but it was home, and I felt comfortable there. At least I tried my hardest to convince myself, considering it was all I could afford after the divorce.

The in-dash clock was illuminated at 11:15. I didn't realize I had been out that long and hadn't even checked my cell phone. Why ruin the good mood I was in to hear some idiotic message left by my ex or, for that matter, anyone. It could wait until tomorrow, and if it was really important, they knew where I lived.

I turned off the highway and slowed down to twenty-five miles per hour. The signs said ten miles per hour, a turtle's crawl, but no one went that slowly anyway except Mrs. Otton with her motorized wheelchair.

I steered onto my street and rolled my car to a stop in front of the trailer under a large palm. I rolled the windows up a crack, almost forgot my cell, went back, grabbed it, and started toward the front door. I was still in a pretty good mood—no, a great mood—for some reason, and then I noticed a light was on in my trailer. I knew for sure I had shut everything off when I left this morning.

Then it dawned on me, Clair! So she had decided to forgive me in her own way, admit she was over-demanding when she had me cornered in the office and decided to come over here to make up. *Hum, I think I'm going to take advantage of this and let her make nice in her own special way. I'll play the man game of hard to get at first; that will leave her wanting to ravage my body even more, thinking she'll need to win me over!* I smiled as the thought of playing for a few hours suddenly put me in the mood.

I slowly opened the unlocked door, had my pissed but surprised look ready, and turned the corner and… what the fuck!

"Okay, who the hell are you guys?"

145

CHAPTER

26

Okay, was I in the right trailer?

I looked around and calmed myself down so I could get my thoughts organized and recognize my surroundings. *Really quick now, think, the table and chairs are mine, the dirty dishes in the sink are from this morning, and that old TV over there is a hand me down. No one gives away good shit, so that's definitely mine. Yeah, I'm in the right place. Okay, let's see now, those two goons in my little living room definitely don't belong to me or anyone I'm acquainted with.*

My heart was beating at a rapid rate, my head spinning, and my good mood quickly disappeared. I still had one foot near the door in case I needed to make a hasty retreat. Damn, I thought to myself, I was really hoping to be having my way with Clair tonight. Oh well, just my typical luck.

"Well, two of the three of us are in the wrong place here, and I know I'm not one of the two," I said in a quick but firm voice. In my younger days, I probably would have been throwing punches by now and taking numbers. But I was smart enough to realize that the odds, along with my age, were not in my favor.

"Mr. Anderson, please have a seat, we need to discuss a few things with you," said the smaller of the two.

As I looked at the two of them, my mind was still in a fuzz. They were inviting me to take a seat in my house? What the...but all of a sudden the guy who just spoke made my mind light up like a neon sign that said, *careful, you've seen this asshole before.*

And I had. It was the guy I met briefly on Mitch's yacht, the one who gave me the eerie feeling by following me around. Come to think about it, he was also the guy who was behind me on the Eau Gallie Causeway, the guy with the familiar car. Mitch also said he didn't really know the guy and had invited him as a favor. So who was the favor for? Was he there to check on me?

He sat there giving off the air of being more important than he probably actually was. He had sandy blond hair and a cleft chin sitting prominently on his small face. He was tall and thinner than a rail. Someone I could easily take if it were just the two of us.

The other guy was the muscle. Tall in stature, he was definitely a gym goon. He also wore a suit, chocolate brown in color, something that looked extremely cheap and should have been at least two sizes larger. Plus it was obvious he was packing. The bulge beneath his jacket was definitely not part of his anatomy.

Something still appeared out of the ordinary. For as much as these two idiots tried to act like city thugs, they still appeared too official for the role.

"You want to discuss something with me? You know you could have knocked on the door or, for that matter, asked me at the party the other night."

This threw the guy off track for a second. It registered on his face that I had recognized him.

"Mr. Anderson," he said, recovering quickly, "we don't have time to make social calls. We were hoping to have a little chat with you and be on our way."

I looked toward the big guy to see his reaction, but there wasn't much of one. He really was acting like the stereotypical goon you read about in books and see on TV. I smiled at him but got nothing in return; probably because his brain couldn't function on any type of higher level.

"Well, I'm really not in the habit of speaking with anyone who breaks into my house," I responded.

He smiled. "Your *house?* Okay, we'll call it that if you like."

Wise ass.

"Mr. Anderson, we are here to deliver a very simple message to you."

"A message, huh? What, you can't pick up the phone or text? I guess he hasn't figured that out yet," I said as I looked toward the muscle, "but you, you look smart enough to handle that."

"Very funny, Mr. Anderson. You pride yourself on your wit and smart ass remarks. I noticed that at the party. Bravo to you."

I stared for a minute; he got me back for that texting remark. Okay, he was pretty witty.

"Let's stop beating around the bush, Mr. Anderson."

I usually tell people to call me Tuck, but not these two assholes and certainly not under these circumstances.

"I repeat, we have a message for you we hope you adhere to for your own safety. We request you drop your investigation of Ed Ventara's last victim and respect the findings of the Brevard County Sheriff's Office."

Okay, here we go again, my mind was winding up like a clock. Why was there so much fuss over a hundred and forty-year-old skeleton and people insisting it was Ventara's victim? And who is "we"? This was nuts!

"Why, Mr....Mr....?" I was hoping he'd follow my cue and give me his name, but he didn't. So I continued, "Because it is not Ventara's last victim."

"With all due respect, Mr. Anderson, you are a reporter, correct? The experts at the sheriff's office have identified the remains as Ventara's, so stop trying to be a hero and let it go."

"With all due respect right back at ya, it is not Ventara's." I stopped short of giving out any additional information.

"Mr. Anderson, I'm not going to sit here and argue with you. The experts have spoken, and that will be the official findings on this case. Honor it!"

"No, I don't think so. I have it on good authority that the remains are not his, and that's a direct quote from Ventara's mouth. The same quote you are going to see reported in the paper."

The big goon smirked at me. "Nice reporting, Mr. Anderson, I'm sure the statement from a convicted— no, a dead convicted—killer who everyone believes took his own life the other day will carry a lot of weight."

Everyone believes? I caught that slip.

The smaller guy gave the muscle a stare that made him cower, and then he looked back at me. The tone of the conversation now changed as he got out of my chair and walked toward the door with the muscle head slinking behind him.

"Mr. Anderson, we have delivered our message, and I am warning you to drop the investigation or—"

"Or else," I smirked.

"If that's what you want to surmise, Mr. Anderson, that's your interpretation, not ours. Just remember you said it, not me. I would definitely sleep with one eye open if I were you, just in case the bed bugs stab you in the freaking heart."

I could have continued the banter for a while longer, but since they were at the door, I'd rather get rid of them. They didn't say another word as they slipped out into the darkness.

I waited a few seconds, slowly walked to the door, peeked out, and saw nothing. They were gone as quickly as they had appeared. I locked the door and checked the windows, closets, and under the bed to ensure my safety—or rather peace of mind.

I turned off all the lights, so if anyone was hanging around in the darkness outside they wouldn't be able to see me inside. I sat at the end of my bed and stared into the abyss.

Again I thought to myself, *what the fuck is going on?* There was so much being made about Osci's poor little child's skeleton.

But why?

I needed more concrete information. I had some ideas, but damn, this was getting complex. My mind was jumbled and I needed time to think.

The evening was cool, and I needed a comforter to warm myself. It would be nice to have Clair's warm butt to rub up against. But, after the conversation we had this afternoon, that was definitely wishful thinking.

As I rested my eyes, I noticed it was 12:45 AM. I could hear a strong breeze blowing through the outside awnings as the trailer creaked.

I laid my head back for a few minutes to think through my plans for tomorrow. Once I had that figured out I placed a baseball bat in bed with me, just to cuddle with, and actually tried to fall asleep with one eye open.

CHAPTER

27

The mist was once again present; it always was in Tucker's dreams. Lightning flashes and the distant rumbles of thunder were more noticeable than in other dreams.

Tucker did not know the location he found himself in, but the sense of familiarity gave him a feeling of comfort. The anxiety he experienced in all his other dreams disappeared. He now accepted and no longer feared his visions. He finally had an understanding; the dreams were a simple means to an end and a message that connected him with his ancestors.

As the mist lifted, a single light became visible in the distance. It drew Tucker toward it and once again he hovered above the water and drifted forward. As the area cleared, he still couldn't put his finger on his exact location. It wasn't the beachside he had become accustomed to in earlier dreams, but rather inland, somewhere along the river.

As he neared the light, things became clearer. The flashes of lightning illuminated a small campfire. A young man sat at the edge of the burning coals. He quickly recognized him as Osci.

Tucker, for the first time, had a clear view of his great-great-uncle. His long hair was raven black, his body tanned and muscular. His face had sharp, distinctive features. The high cheekbones, slim nose, and wide, almond-shaped eyes gave him a unique look. Tucker was astounded to see his ancestor at such close range.

Osci sat cross-legged with the palms of his hands resting on his knees. Tucker was drawn to the opposite side of the fire and came to rest on a small log. He froze as he noticed a very large alligator resting at Osci's side. It didn't move, but lay with its snout forward and its eyes—yes, its eyes—locked on Tucker. This unnerved Tucker for just a second as the gator's eyes glistened to a bright red and its jaw seemed to take the outline of a dangerous smile.

The trance broke when Osci spoke. It was the first time Tucker had heard a sound uttered from his uncle. The voice was deep, clear, and sure of itself.

"My nephew," Osci started. "You are my chosen one. Every soul is connected through time and space with another. You are one with me. You are the embodiment of everything I was." Osci raised his hands to the sky, then paused and took a long, hard look at Tucker, who sat and listened but, for the first time in his life, had nothing to say.

"Our family has endured many hardships over time. I need you to understand that."

He gazed at Tucker, and Tucker nodded his head yes in acknowledgment. He went on. "Some hardships have been more difficult than others, but to each spirit they are an important part of their history. I have suffered much pain, but none can be harder to bear than the loss of my child. "

Again he stopped and looked at Tucker. Their eyes locked. For a moment, Tucker felt as if he was looking into the mirror of his soul.

"I understand," Tucker finally said.

Tucker knew deep down he could never truly understand the sadness of losing a child. Just the thought of losing his own was heart wrenching. But it did give him an understanding as to why his uncle was not able to rest in peace.

Osci nodded.

"I still can't figure out what you want me to do," replied Tucker. "I know the skeleton on the beachside was your son, and I'm sorry for that. I have also told a number of people the remains are not of another and plan on reporting those facts as need be, so everyone is informed." Tucker stopped, not knowing what else to say.

"What I want," Osci began, "is for my son to be returned to me and the murderer punished. "

Tucker was stunned. How in the world could he have his son's remains returned and punish the murderer?

The question lingered in Tucker's eyes and Osci answered for him. "I want my son's remains to be buried here." Osci raised his arms again. As he did so, the gator's head lifted and looked at Tucker.

"This is now the resting place of my family. Crystal, my son's mother, and I need to be placed together so we can rest in eternal peace. "

"I understand," Tucker answered. "Getting the remains of your child is something I might be able to do, but how is

the murderer, who died many years ago, to be punished today? That I simply do not understand."

Osci smiled. "As I said, my boy, all souls are connected. Good or evil, all have a connection through time and space. As I have with you, so our murderer is connected with another from your generation."

Tucker sat in deep thought. "Okay, you need me to find someone who is connected with your murderer and do what, retaliate?"

Osci again smiled. "My nephew, there is a plan for everything. Every soul has a course to follow. You have your direction, which has been shaped over time."

Tucker once again looked confused.

"You are a writer of words to many people, are you not?" Osci smiled. "You have the ability with the written word to bring shame and dishonor to our family's enemies. That is what I want you to do."

Tucker sat quietly again not knowing what to say and afraid to say anything. He sat deep in thought. "My uncle, I will do my best to accomplish what you ask. I will honor your wishes and venture to do my best to fulfill them."

From behind Tucker a voice drifted through the mist.

"Tucker, my love."

His hairs stood up on the back of his neck as he heard the familiar voice.

"You must carry out the wishes of your uncle. He needs you now. Remember, Tucker, without family, there is nothing."

Tucker knew the voice and spun around. Tears began to flow as the sight of Nana before him sent him to his knees.

"Nan...please, not you!" Tucker cried out.

"Shh, it's okay, my love. My time has come. Please do not cry over me. Your family and I now need you to complete this journey. I will lead you to its completion when the time comes."

* * *

Thunder boomed and lightning flashed as Tucker awoke with tears in his eyes at the ringing of his cell phone.

He rolled to his side and glanced at the clock. He picked up the phone, already knowing what the message would be.

"Mr. Anderson," the voice spoke softly. "This is Holms Regional Medical Center calling. We are sorry to inform you that Gladys Lee Anderson passed away at 12:45 this morning. Sorry it took so long to contact you. We needed to contact the director of the assisted living manor for her next of kin."

Tucker glanced at the time again. It was 2:22. He said thank you and rolled onto his back. It was the first time in his adult life that he cried like a child. The last time he felt like this was the day his mother left.

CHAPTER

28

A cloudy, damp Tuesday welcomed the new morning to Central Florida. I lay in bed, drifting in and out of sleep, followed by the occasional tears. The thoughts washing through my mind were all of Nan. She had been my rock. The one who calmed me when I was upset, punished me when I misbehaved as a child, and comforted me when times were bad. Without a doubt, she was always my biggest fan. We had a very special relationship; much more than grandmother and grandson. She disciplined me yet at the same time was a good friend. Her advice was always sound, and her relentless attitude of never settling for less than the best was built into my psyche.

The loss of her was going to be hard. I had always feared the day she would be taken from me, but to be honest, after last night I found solace knowing I would always be connected with her, even if it just happened through my dreams.

I left the house and headed down to Melbourne to take care of Nan's arrangements. I knew what her wishes were and planned on carrying them out to the letter. I also planned on carrying out Osci's wishes as best I could.

My mind was made up, and when I set my mind to something, I made things happen. I did it with all my energy. I figured I could honor Osci's request for the remains. I'd steal them if I had to. I wasn't sure, however, how to carry out Osci's requests for retaliation, but I would figure that out as I went along.

I arrived at the assisted living complex after I completed all the paperwork at Holms Medical Center to make sure all loose ends were tied up and all of Nan's friends knew she was in a better place.

She had no desire to have a viewing and be gawked at. She always joked that if she were laid out for people to see, regardless of what others thought, to just lay her face down so everyone could kiss her ass goodbye. Her true wishes were to be cremated and her ashes scattered over marshland she owned west of I-95.

That was Nan. No bullshit. She pulled no punches, and that quality remained endearing to me. Thinking of all this brought a smile to my face as I walked into the complex.

Room seventeen was just as I had left it the other day. Everything was neat and in its place. The staff had all of Nan's precious pictures and knickknacks boxed on the table. Everything else, as requested, would be donated to charity.

A letter sat on top of the box with my name printed neatly in Nan's handwriting.

I picked it up slowly and held it for a second. It almost seemed as if she knew her time had come and left it for me to read.

It read:

Tucker, my love,

If you are reading this, I have already left on my journey to join our family. Please don't be upset, just know that we will always be connected beyond space and time.

Tucker, since you were a little boy, I knew we shared a special bond, it goes deeper than our blood connection, something much more spiritual. I have watched you grow from a child to the wonderful man you are today. You are very special to me, more than my words can ever express. I ask that whenever you feel lonely, please remember how much I love you and how important you have been in my life. You have been a constant source of happiness for me, and I enjoyed every minute of our time together.

Remember, Tucker, you are a unique person with special abilities. Because of your strong energy, you can make connections with your past that others are not open to.

We will be together again, my love, but at this time, I have to be on my way. Never forget, Tucker, I love you!

~Nan

The letter was bittersweet. My eyes burned as they swelled with tears. Though she never said it, I knew she loved me, and having her for part of my life was a gift I would forever cherish.

I folded the note, placed it in my pocket, wiped a few more tears from my eyes, grabbed the box, and headed for the door. Before leaving, I turned and found the dream catcher still hanging in the window. I walked over, took it down, and placed it in the box I carried.

I left room seventeen holding my head high and smiling with a warm feeling in my soul. I was proud to be the grandson of Gladys Lee Anderson.

CHAPTER

29

As I walked to my car, the sun started to break through the low covering of clouds. A light appeared to brighten my path. I looked up, smiled, and said, "Thank you, Nan."

I placed the box gently in the back of my Cherokee and all of a sudden had an eerie feeling I was being watched. The nerve endings in my body made my hairs stand on end. I turned to my left and caught a glimpse of a sedan passing by. Inside were the two goons who had invaded my home. They weren't aware I saw them, and I played the sighting off as nonchalantly as I could.

Okay, enough of this shit. I've had it. These mother fuckers are going to get it, I said to myself as I ran a number of scenarios over and over again in my mind. But now was not the place and time to be concerned with them. That time would come. I now needed to be very deliberate in my choices. The two goons had to be working for some-one, and that someone had something to do with the remains from the beachside.

I left the assisted living home, figured I would take the short ride over to the library and check out a hunch I'd been thinking about since the other day.

Upon arriving at the library, I passed through the sliding glass doors and immediately walked to the chil-dren's section in hopes of finding Mrs. C. She wasn't there. I quietly walked between the stack of books and eyed the long aisles in hopes of finding her. A few women spotted me peeking around the corners from a stack of books and gave me dirty looks. Apparently I was disturbing their silent reading. I even heard one woman call me a pervert. *Hum...guess she knows me*, I thought to myself and smiled, giving her a wink while she gave me the finger. Oh well.

At the counter, I waited a few minutes to speak to the clerk Mrs. C had pointed out to me as someone helpful. She looked cute, but not really my type. When I approached, an immediate smile came to her face.

Oh shit, I thought, *Mrs. C has been trying to set me up again*.

"Hi, my name is Tucker and I'm—"

"A friend of Mrs. C," she completed.

"Yes, yes, I am. By chance is she here today?" I politely smiled.

"Oh, I am sorry Mr. Tucker—"

"Please, it's just Tucker," I replied.

I saw her blush. "Mrs. C is off today, but I'm sure I can help you with whatever you might need."

I thanked her and said I knew where to go and appreciated her taking the time to talk with me and to tell Mrs. C I had stopped in to see her.

"Okay, Tucker," she said and smiled. "I'll tell her. Oh, by the way, did your two friends find you the other day?"

This made me freeze for a second as I knew who the two friends she mentioned were, so I tried to calmly play it out. "My two friends from the other day?" I chimed in.

"Yes," she said. "They came in right after you left and wanted to make sure you found the information you had come in looking for. Mrs. C, being the outstanding librarian she is, helped by showing them the exact same maps you were looking at."

Son of a bitch.

"Just to make sure," I said, "you mean my old buddies Tom and Bill." I made up the names. "One is skinny, kind of tall with blonde hair, and the other, Bill, is kind of big and stout?"

"Yes, that's them. Very nice guys and professional looking too," she agreed.

I went on. "Could you show me the maps they were looking at? I want to make sure we're all on the same page with our information."

"Sure, give me a second and I'll show you."

I followed her back to the research section and was shown a large book of maps I actually hadn't taken the time to look through the other day.

"Hope this helps you, let me know if you need anything else," she said with a smile and excused herself.

I have to be honest. I did check her out as she walked away, and you know what, not too bad. She had a cute little body, but still not my type.

I zeroed in on the atlas and the pages I was shown. They were old maps of Brevard and, to be specific, Merritt Island, dating back to the mid-1800s. I focused long and hard on the map until I was satisfied with what I had seen. The name listed was exactly what I thought it would be.

Damn, why hadn't I figured this out earlier? It was a shock, but I wasn't totally surprised. I needn't look any further as my mind was clear, and what I needed to do was starting to make sense.

I closed the large, cumbersome book and worked my way over to the computers. No more than thirty minutes allowed, the notice read as I signed in to use computer number five. Once I was signed on, it only took me a few minutes to search for the name I was interested in.

I'll be damned, I said to myself. *I never knew that name was so involved with the history and early development of life here in Brevard.* Again, shocked? No, just surprised, hell yes—surprised.

30

Heading back to my parking spot, a feeling of satisfaction came over me. With a clearing sky and soft breeze blowing in from the east, I believed I now knew why there was so much interest in the beachside skeleton. To be honest, I could care less about that, and I could easily forget about it if the goons had not threatened my space. The concern I now had revolved around how I was going to reunite Osci and his family. I had an idea that would take a lot of work, but it was worth a try.

I looked over and saw I had a number of messages on my cell and was about to check them when my phone almost jumped out of my hand. The ring startled me.

"Tucker speaking."

"Hello, Tucker." It was Marion.

"Yes, Marion, what can you do me for?" I wise cracked.

"Tucker, I didn't call to argue with you. Charles and I just wanted to let you know how sorry we are Nan passed. I know how much she meant to you," she said sincerely.

How the hell did she find out so quickly?

"Thank you, Marion, but how did you find out? I haven't told the kids yet."

"Charles was on call last night at Holms and he recognized the name when it came across his desk. That is his job, you know."

Okay, I could have been a wise ass and made a comment that would have gotten her pissed off, but you know, it's just not worth it anymore.

"Thank you," I answered. "I appreciate the call."

"Hold on, Tucker, the kids are here and want to speak with you."

I wasn't too sure what to say to Carl or how he would deal with death at his age, so I really didn't want to keep him on too long and get him upset. Jessie, on the other hand, was truly heartbroken. She had been more involved with Nan at an early age than her brother had been before the divorce. Before Nan became confined to her wheelchair, Jessie used to spend countless hours on Nan's lap listening to her stories.

"Daddy," Jessie cried. "I am so, so sorry to hear our Nana is gone. She...she was—" I could hear her breathing, but her voice was barely coming through the phone as it started to crack. "She was one of my favorite people."

"I know, hon, she was someone special," I tried to calm her a little. "I just know she'll be watching over you and your brother. She loved you guys very much."

"I …I know, Daddy, Dad…I love you very much!"

"I know you do. You will always be my little girl. Do me a favor and watch over your brother, I'll call you guys later on."

I paused for a moment to reflect. They were pretty good kids, and you know what? With Nan and them, my family wasn't too bad.

I decided to check the rest of my messages. Two of them where from Marion and the kids, but the other was a total surprise.

Beep. "Hi, Tucker, I don't know if you remember me, but it's Karla, a good friend of Craig's. Could you please give me a call, it's very important I speak with you. My number is…"

I stored her number into my phone memory and quickly dialed Craig's cell. I wanted to make sure I wasn't in for any surprises.

"Hello…"

"Hey, Craig," I started and then was cut off.

"This is Craig, I can't answer my cell right now, but if it's important, well, you're out of luck." He laughed as the message beeped off.

Very funny, I thought. Nice to see after all these years he still had a sense of humor. As teens, he was always the quieter one. He was the one that pulled all the pranks I got blamed for. Many times in school he got me so pissed that I was ready to beat the crap out of him, but as soon as he saw me, he would double over in laughter about my getting blamed. I couldn't stay mad at him, and I too would just end up laughing with him.

His best scheme was one night when he got us to go alligator hunting. Yes, you heard me, alligator hunting. If it weren't for the fact we were drunk off our asses and the gator only a four-foot baby, I would never have been involved in such of a stunt.

Well, then again, who am I trying to kid? I probably still would have done it.

Anyway, a gator had been reported in a local retention basin. Most of the time, unless the wildlife is a direct threat to humans, nothing is done about it. That's where we came in. We baited the little guy. We got him in a position so we could get our weight on him—or should I say my weight on him. Duck taped his mouth and covered his claws as we laid him in the back of Craig's pickup and made our way to the high school. There we tied the gator to the base of the flagpole with a dog chain and leash. It was a great welcome gift for the staff and students as they arrived for school the next morning. Needless to say, this caused a lot of commotion, and we were questioned and released by our principal, never to be proven guilty. We laughed for days, but I think the questioning part of that investigation got Craig interested in the law. To serve and protect, he cried out whenever we got drunk on the beach.

That thought brought a smile to my face and made me laugh out loud as I dialed up his office. Craig had really turned out to be the ultimate professional. Who would have thought?

"Hello, sheriff's office," a sweet voice answered.

"Hi, could I please speak to Craig Lanton?"

"Who may I say is calling," she asked.

"This is Tucker Anderson, Craig is a personal friend of mine, and if you could just say it's me, he's expecting my call."

"Please hold, I'll connect you."

After a minute she returned, "I'm sorry, Detective Lanton is out on assignment. I'll connect you with his superior if you like."

Hold on here. Out on assignment? We had agreed to stay in touch and trade information. He wouldn't not call me, especially if he was away on assignment. Why would she say a superior would call me? That would be someone I didn't know and who didn't know me. I decided I wanted out of this call now.

I punched in Karla's number.

"Tucker," she responded on answering. "I need to talk with you. Craig gave me your number and asked me to contact you."

"On the phone or in person?" I asked.

"I'd rather we get together."

"Fine, where do you want to meet?"

"I get off at four o'clock; let's meet over at the port. There's a lot of traffic and it's a good place where we can blend in and not be seen."

"How will I find you?" I asked.

"Don't worry, Craig described your car. I'll find you." She hung up.

I finally got on the road and headed north, and my cell phone rang out again.

"Tucker, this is Mitch, I need to see you in my office, now!"

CHAPTER

31

"Mitch! You have to be shitting me!"

Mitch just sat there in a trance. I had a side view of him as he sat in his chair facing the windows that overlooked a majestic palm and the parking lot.

"Mitch! Are you listening?"

"Tuck...Tuck...I really don't know what to tell you. All I know is that we—you—have to drop the investigation over the beachside skeleton."

I moved toward Mitch's desk and grabbed the edges as my knuckles turned white from pressure. I leaned my chest in as much as I could, without being too threatening.

"Mitch, you know this is bullshit," I said in a firm and steady voice. "Be upfront with me and give me the real reason you want this dropped. After all these years, you at least owe me that."

Mitch took a deep breath and swiveled his chair around to square off with me. "Okay, Tucker, you want to know why? Well...well," he stuttered, "I need to protect this paper. It's been in my family for generations and I am not going to be the one who loses it."

I looked at him funny. "Lose it? How the hell could you possibly lose it?"

Mitch attempted to look at me but his eyes darted away. "Tucker, this paper is in the red. More than it should be."

"You're saying the paper owes money? So what, every company owes money to someone." I gave him one more look before I pulled away from his desk and took a seat. The intensity our conversation started with lessened. Mitch just sat there like a berated little school boy. His eyes stared at the floor.

"Hold on here." I stopped as a thought entered my mind. "Don't tell me you've been skimming off the top?"

He didn't even have to respond. The look on his face said it all. I actually started to feel sorry for him.

"Tucker, look at me. Look at the life I live. Do you really think I could afford my lifestyle and be married to the woman I am without the extra money?"

He had a great salary, but damn, what a bad judge of finance and obvious low self-esteem. I have to be honest, though, I always knew it was the money that kept his wife around. I couldn't see any other reason for her being with him. Look what his money got him in college— the hottie from the corrections facility.

Mitch went on, "I'm not you, Tucker, I'm not the jock you are who can keep women interested without the cash. I've always admired you and would love to just trade places with you for a single day."

Wow, I was taken back. I always thought he felt that way, but to hear his admission shocked the hell out of me.

"I've gotten in too deep, way over my head, and I can't lose this paper because of my stupid mistakes. If that happens, I lose everything, not just my lifestyle, but my family too."

Now it was my turn to sit in silence. I stared out the window as the big billowy November clouds set shadows across the parking lot and through the room.

"Mitch," I said cautiously, "I never knew. Wow, I guess—" And then I was back to normal. "Wait a minute! How the hell does this paper's finances affect the beachside investigation?"

Before he could answer, it dawned on me. Son of a bitch, that name. Now it all made sense to me, but I wasn't going to say anything to Mitch just yet.

Mitch answered, "I've been told by our board of trustees and the bank that we need to drop the investigation. I didn't ask why, and I honestly don't know why. I was just told to do it, and from their tone, I know they mean business, especially when they threatened to call in the loans I owe on the paper if the investigation didn't cease. Tucker, I can't let that happen."

Honestly, I did care about Mitch and his problems, but I wasn't going to let it interfere with what I needed to do for my family. But without Mitch and the paper, there was no way for me to get my story out.

Then I decided to spin the table and change my approach. "Listen, Mitch, I'm surprised at the way you're acting right now," I said in an encouraging voice.

He looked at me quizzically as I continued, "I never in a million years figured you'd back down from a challenge and abandon a teammate. That's not the Mitch and award-winning journalist I know." I started slowly to get up and leave.

"Wait, what do you mean by that?" Mitch came back quickly.

I knew him all too well; I had him with the jock angle. "You just surprise me, that's all. You should know a teammate never, no matter how beat up he is, ever lets his other teammates down. When things get tough, a real player meets the challenge. The team comes together, digs deep. and together we get it done!"

Mitch's eyes widened.

"And you know what, Mitch, we never, ever back down. When it's fourth and inches or time is running off the clock and we need a basket, you've got to be able to step up and carry your teammates on your back, but I guess you're…"

Mitch was now on the edge of his seat.

"…But I guess you're not the teammate I thought you were. I never thought you would step away from the plate and walk away without at least a fight and to just let someone push you aside, it's insulting."

You could actually see the light bulb click. I started to walk to the door when Mitch finally spoke. "You're wrong, Tuck, you are my teammate and no one pushes our team around!"

He got out of his chair and started to pace back and forth. I couldn't help but grin. "Tucker, no one tells us what to do. You're my buddy, and we always fight together, I got your back," he said as he paced himself into a trance. "When the going gets tough, the tough get going." He pepped himself up. "But Tucker, you're the captain, what do you think we should do?"

"I'll be your captain, Mitch, and your fullback, but you're the quarterback and the brains of the team." I needed to make him think he was in charge, even though I'd be calling all the shots. "What play do you want to run to win this game?" I knew that would get him.

He smiled. "This is what we'll do. You continue to investigate on the QT, and I'll tell everyone the investigation is over. But Tucker, you need to tie this up quickly so we can hit them with a three-pointer." He smiled as his posture changed, and he visually became more self-assured.

"That's good, that's real good," I said, boosting his confidence. "And since I might be being watched, I'll leave here all pissed off, slamming some doors to give our plan some teeth."

He smiled and stuck out his hand for a firm shake. "Teammates," he repeated.

"You better believe it," I said as we shook and gave each other a quick man hug. I gave him a wink and headed to the door, raising my voice as I opened it. "This is pure bullshit, Mitch!" I yelled loud enough to get everyone's attention. "I've had enough of your crap," and slammed the door on my out.

"What the hell are you looking at?" I shouted at a copy boy as everyone slithered away from me as I walked through the office. I opened the side door, stepped out into the clean, cool air, and smiled. Sometimes, even I impress myself.

CHAPTER

32

I left the building with a sense of satisfaction and the promise of dreams to be fulfilled. I was determined to have this all work out. The one main attribute I got from Nan was her stubbornness. If someone told me not to do something, I was more inclined to do it, just to prove I could.

The weather had cleared nicely and the crispness of the air put a new hop in my step. Thinking of Nan gave me a momentarily lapse into sorrow, but also having the knowledge she was still near made me feel a lot more at ease.

I got to my Cherokee, looked around, saw no one, jumped in, and headed out to meet Karla.

I headed out on U.S. 1 and decided to take a longer loop around to reach Jetty Park at the cape. I took the cut-off leading me west to I-95. I planned on heading north to rebound onto 528 and then east to Cape Canaveral.

I was positive by the time I approached I-95 that no one was following. This gave me a moment of satisfaction, but the question still lingered in my mind as to how the goons somehow always ended up nearby. This was really starting to bother me.

Then it dawned on me. I pulled the car over into a Hess gas station right before I-95. I pulled off my Oakleys, opened the door, and laid myself across the front seat and started to search underneath it.

Nothing—shit.

It had to be here somewhere. I lay on my back and started to search underneath the dash, and lo and behold, there it was. Why didn't I think of this earlier? A damn tracking device was under there, about the size of a domino and stuck with a magnet under my dash. Normally I wouldn't even know what one looked like, but Craig and I had played a joke on a few girls back in high school and they're easy to get.

You asshole, I said to myself. I should have known something was up when I got into the car the other day and my seat was moved.

Oh well, no reason to get all worked up now. I removed the tracking device, smiled, and looked around. I figured they weren't close enough for me to see them since I now knew what they looked like. My grin grew wider as I took the device and placed it under a car with New Jersey tags.

"That should keep them busy for a while. Hope those assholes follow the car all the way to the Georgia line," I said to myself as I jumped in and headed onto I-95.

I zoomed up the interstate and exited onto 528, with not much traffic. It was only a short time before I crossed the causeway with the cruise liners hovering in port to my left. The little mouse had his ship there along with a number of others. Wow, the port had really grown since the days of the space race. It was now one of the largest ports for cruises, other than Miami, on the East Coast.

I looped around and took George King Boulevard and weaved my way through the port to Jetty Maritime Park. I parked, threw on my baseball cap, and took a leisurely stroll toward the jetty as I checked my cell for messages. Nothing, good. No news is good news.

Karla said she would find me, so I played the part of a tourist and found a nice bench overlooking the grounds to do a little people watching.

My mind drifted back and forth between happy thoughts of Nan and what I was planning when, all of a sudden, I felt a tap on my shoulder. I turned, but could only see the silhouette of a woman, backed by palms and a mix of sun and clouds.

"Tucker?" she questioned.

"Yes." I stood and moved to get a better angle so I could see her face. "Karla?"

"Yes, I am sorry, have you been waiting long?" she asked.

At about five feet nine inches with curves that accented her tight jeans, she was striking, to say the least. Long dark hair, pulled through a baseball cap, and large oval sunglasses framed a face tan in color with a beautiful smile that put you completely at ease.

"No, not very," I stammered.

She smiled in return as she looked over her shoulder with caution. "Craig wanted me to meet you. Though we're no longer the item we once were, he's still my closest friend and he explained everything to me."

I didn't answer but let her continue as we started a stroll around the grounds.

"I did work on the beachside skeleton and believe me, there is no way in hell that's Ventara's. I personally have seen his work, and if you have seen a deceased child, believe me, it's something you never forget. Plus the bone analysis dates the skeleton to over one hundred years old."

"I know," I said, agreeing.

We paused, and she looked at me again, lifted her glasses, and smiled. "I'll cut to the chase," she said. "Craig did fill me in on your involvement here, and if need be I have no problems getting the remains for you. They would only end up as fertilizer somewhere anyway. I can replace them, and no one would be the wiser."

I could easily see why Craig had once been involved with such a woman. Being extremely smart and attractive was bad enough, but her personality, the way she spoke, and the way she handled herself, gave her a beauty that radiated throughout her person. I was in total awe. Karla was without a doubt a woman that any normal male couldn't pass up.

We walked and talked and covered every detail of the case a while longer as the shadows started to extend over the park. A slight breeze came off the ocean and rustled the palms as the temperature started to change.

The plans were made for me to arrive at the justice complex in Rockledge tomorrow afternoon for the pick-up. I was actually upset that our short time together was coming to an end.

"Karla, I can't thank you enough for what you're doing. You don't even know me that well, yet you're willing to stick your neck out for me. I really don't know how to thank you."

"Don't say anything," she blushed. "You being Craig's best friend is enough for me, plus the few times we met was always enjoyable for me," she said with a smile. She continued, "Craig and I know something isn't kosher here, and dirty politics seems to be involved somehow. We both decided something had to be corrected, especially when things started to go sour like this. Craig will call you shortly. He still doesn't understand why he's being watched so closely."

I laughed. "I'll talk to him. It's not him, it's me. It's the price he's paying for being my friend. I'll even that account out shortly."

I thanked her again, took a chance and kissed her on the cheek and said my good-byes. We went our separate ways. I decided to hit P.J.'s up for a bite to eat and a cold beer.

I walked into P.J.'s and immediately caught the raised eyebrows of Andy. When he saw me enter, he motioned for me to sit at the far end of the bar, and I did. He brought me a beer and wasted no time filling me in.

"Tucker, it seems you're the popular guy around town."

I waited for his smile, which never came. He was dead serious.

"Let me guess." I smiled. "Two guys have been asking about me, a tall, thin guy and Mr. Pro Body Builder, both wearing suits that don't fit," I said with a snicker in my voice.

"Trophy to the winner. These somewhat official-looking guys waved some bullshit credentials at me and said I better not hold anything back."

"Well, I know you didn't, so I guess what you don't know won't hurt you," I replied.

"Tucker, seriously, you okay?" he asked with concern in his voice. "If you need anything, I've got you covered. Just give me a holler." He winked and went to wait on another customer.

I spent a good couple of hours at the bar. Had a nice fish wrap, some fries, and two more beers to complete my dinner. I sat in wonder as to how in just less than one week my entire life had changed. I had a nice routine going and now, well, now I felt as if I were a child suddenly thrust into adulthood.

I took the usual route home and thought about my plans for tomorrow. Pulling up to my trailer, I was sure to check and see if any lights were on. Seeing none, I parked my faithful means of transportation at the curb and made my way toward the front door. The door was locked, which was strange. I never left it locked. There was nothing of real value in there. I started to fumble with my keys when I remembered my cell and headed back to the car.

The explosion lit up the Central Brevard area and could be seen as far away as Honeymoon Lake. Car alarms sounded, sirens wailed, dogs barked, and women screamed at the sight of the fireball that illuminated the trailer park. With the wind knocked out of me, I was able to crawl to the curbside next to the Cherokee. The last thing I remembered was a young teen asking if I was okay right before I blacked out.

A lone man sat in his car with his finger next to the button. No one seemed to be hurt, which was fine. Hopefully the message was conveyed loud and clear. He placed the remote on the seat next to him and slowly pulled his sedan away from the curb and out of the park.

CHAPTER

33

Blackness, total blackness, and then a light at the end of the tunnel.

Voices, muffled voices. I couldn't understand what was being said. Was someone calling me? *Is that you, Nan? Am I dead?*

I tried to move toward the light, but felt as if a greater force was holding me back. The light started to flash and move side to side as the voices started to become clearer.

"Sir, can you hear me? Follow the light, look at it. Now try and fully open those eyes."

As I slowly regained consciousness, I realized an EMS worker had me propped up against the curb checking me for a concussion and other injuries.

"Watch my finger, follow it. You'll be okay. That was one hell of a blast you had there." I finally understood something he had said.

"It must have been your propane tank that leaked."

"My place is...was all electric," I said. "Damn, my head hurts, how long have I been out of it?"

"I don't know. When we arrived you were sprawled out on the grass."

I turned my head and looked back at the carnage that was once my home. Smoke still drifted in the air and the smell of fire burned my nostrils. Even my landscaping was gone. I was so proud of those palms I had planted by hand, and now they were all singed and looked like tall toothpicks in the sand. The firefighters were still spraying water on the surrounding trailers; a few had melted siding, but luckily for them, mine was the only one that exploded.

Emergency vehicles lined the roadway as police held my curious neighbors at bay, questioning a few.

I rose to my feet. I felt a little wobbly and quickly sat back down, fearing I'd pass out if I didn't. I knew I just needed a few more minutes to shake out the cobwebs in my head.

"Hey, Tucker." A familiar voice and a silhouette came jogging out of the misty smoke. It was Craig.

"Man, you're a sight for sore eyes," I stated. "Where the hell have you been?"

Craig came over and gave me a hug and looked me over, then looked back at the trailer. "I heard the call over the radio and heard your address. I got here as quickly as I could. They sent me on some bullshit task force up to Volusia," he responded. "You'll be all right, you've taken a lot worse hits than this and got right back up on your feet." He grinned, then his entire posture changed and he looked at me seriously.

"Tucker, whatever you need to do, I've got your back. Something is really rotten here, and I'm not one hundred percent sure where it's headed, but it now needs to be brought out in the open. Seeing this tonight, whoever they are went way too far."

"Buddy, yes, it has gone way too far, and I need to finish this, but I don't want you putting your career on the line for me," I said, placing the ice pack the EMS guy handed me on the back of my neck.

"My career," he said with a laugh. "Don't worry about it. I had a long talk with my commander this evening."

"How'd that go?"

He smirked. "Pretty good, I started mentioning obstruction of justice and shit like that and he eyed me up for a while then finally said, get the fuck out of my office. Right then, I knew something weird was up, but I truly believe he has no idea either. He's just following orders."

Without warning I turned and found Mitch standing at my side. It looked as if he was about to cry. Craig also noticed him and quickly said, "I'll talk to you tomorrow, we'll catch up," then turned and walked over to the investigators.

"Tucker, I don't know what to say," Mitch struggled to get out.

"Don't say anything, man, I'm alive," I said and gave him a slap on the back.

"You're my teammate, Tuck, whatever you need from me, just mention it," he said seriously.

"Well, a place to stay would be a nice gesture," I answered half-heartedly.

"Excuse me, gentlemen, but we better get you to the hospital to get checked out," the EMS attendant said.

I looked at him, thought for a moment, and said, "No thanks, I'm fine. I don't need no stinking hospital to tell me that." Actually the idea wasn't a bad one with all things considered. I had no place to sleep or food to eat, but I knew I'd be stuck there much longer than needed, and I didn't want to get into all the paperwork.

"Well, if you're sure," the attendant went on, "I need you to sign off, saying you know it all and refuse treatment."

I doubt it said *I know it all,* but I signed and refused. I slowly started to walk with Mitch. We stopped and just stared at what was once my trailer.

"Things are getting interesting," I said, looking at Mitch with a raised eyebrow.

"About having a place to stay," Mitch started, "I want you to take the keys to the sailboat, it's yours for as long as you want it or I have it."

"Mitch, I can't—"

"No, Tuck, I'm not giving you an option, I demand you use it. It's fully stocked and wanting to be used."

"Well, if you insist…" I'd be a fool to turn this down.

"And Tucker, I'm with you more than one hundred percent, just please be careful and get this over with ASAP."

The area had just about cleared out. Craig had taken care of the police reports, and all the neighbors had gone back into their homes. Yeah, yeah, I know, they're just trailers, as my ex-wife would joke.

Mitch and I stood alone. "Mitch, thank you. You are truly a teammate in every sense of the word."

"Get going," he said emotionally, "you could use the sleep."

I took the keys to the "yacht" and started toward the Cherokee, sadly the only thing I still owned.

"Hey, Tuck," Mitch yelled. "You know Clair is really a nice girl and a hell of a catch. She went over to the boat and got things ready for you."

Damn, he'd known about the office romance all along, I thought as I drove away. Guess I'm not as discreet as I thought I was.

The drive down to the marina didn't take long. The road was clear with very little traffic. I found the reserved spot for Mitch's yacht and walked down the dock. The boat gently rocked in its slip with the sound of buckles clanging the mast. I stepped on board, being careful with my step, still feeling a little wobbly from the blast, and worked my way to the master suite. The bed was a welcome sight as I undressed, slid myself under the smooth satin sheets and fell immediately into a deep sleep.

CHAPTER

34

Did you ever wake up and have the feeling you were in one place and then realized you were actually someplace else? That was me. It wasn't in a bad way I felt this way, not like after a long night on the town and waking up in some strange bed…Not that there is anything wrong with that or that I've done that or anything. Hmm…

Well anyway, I awoke around ten with that feeling, but it was quite the contrary—a good one, a feeling that I belonged here. I slept soundly and opened my eyes and felt well rested, sore, but well rested. My mind was clear and I felt great—mentally, that is.

I had a number of dreams, nothing detailed as in the past, but a number of them: playing with my kids, Nan and I walking before age took over her body, Osci smiling at me from his canoe, nodding his head yes and wanting me to follow him, and even one of my dad and me when I was very young; a sad but happy time for me. The dreams were all short clips but feel-good ones.

I got up with a little stretch and worked my way to the galley to see if Mitch had any coffee stored on board. There was, along with the note from Clair.

Tucker,

I am so relieved you are okay. Mitch called me and told me what happened, so I took the time to do some quick shopping for you this morning. You'll find everything you need in the fridge and pantry. I also stopped at Beall's and picked you up a few pairs of shorts, shirts, and the essentials you'll need until you find the time to shop.

I know we haven't quite been ourselves lately, but I also know I care for you deeply and will always be here for you when you need me.

We'll talk soon,
Clair

That was nice of her. Mitch was right, she was a great girl.

I found the coffee and set the dial to brew. The rich Blue Mountain aroma immediately filled the cabin and smelled great. I took my cup of coffee and found my way back to the stateroom. This really was a beautiful yacht. The amenities here outdid most homes I've seen.

I found the clothes Clair had picked up and took a long hot shower. I let the warm water soak its way under my skin to the sore spots along my back. Being sore brought back memories of how it felt to be beat up after I played a hard-fought game. This was definitely the game of my life.

I dressed, brushed my hair back, and headed through the cabin up onto the deck. It was a gorgeous morning. Big puffy clouds and a little warmer than it should be. The marina was still quiet, but you could hear the clanging of the buckles on the masts as the boats rocked gently back and forth in their slips.

"Ahoy there, matey," came a voice from the next dock.

I walked to the side rail, shading my eyes from the sun, sipping away at my coffee. "Ahoy there to you," I yelled back.

"Beautiful morning," came the answer from the guy down from New Jersey who I had met at Mitch's party. He walked over and said, "Permission to come aboard."

"Permission granted," I replied, but honestly, this whole dialogue was getting corny to me.

"Mitch gave me the heads-up last night that you'd be here, so I took the liberty to pick up a few rolls and pastries as a welcoming gift."

We sat on the cushioned captain's chairs in the rear of the boat. It was clear from the ease of our conversation that Doug and I were quickly becoming friends. Though there seemed to be a big age difference, he was a cool guy.

We traded life's stories and laughed quite a bit. Doug had sailed for years. He had taken the time now, at the age of sixty-five, to enjoy himself. He sold everything he didn't lose in his divorce, bought himself a nice sailboat, then did what most men dream of—sailed away. After his bitter divorce up north he found it easy to leave. He was an accomplished sailor and spent a year and a half sailing the Caribbean from the Bahamas to Barbados, all on his own, except for the occasional "young female" companion, as he put it, who needed a lift to the next island. He had some great stories, and I enjoyed listening to him. He had decided to set up a mooring in Melbourne and stay for a while.

Time flew by, and before we knew it, it was a little after twelve. We made plans to trade stories again, but this time with a few beers rather than coffee. It remained to be seen, but I think I had a new friend.

I made my way below deck again, looking for my cell. Thinking it must be in my car, I got myself ready for the final phase of my journey. As I grabbed my keys and made my way to the car, I remembered that it was actually my cell that saved my life. Sure glad I left it in the car.

I passed a few of Mitch's friends and took a minute to introduce myself as they eyed me with suspicion. This marina wasn't a place for strangers to stroll through, which actually made me feel better. They would keep an eye out, questioning anyone who didn't belong.

I turned out of the marina and headed north, and I quickly noticed a familiar sight. A dark sedan pulled out to join me, which was just fine, since I was hoping to see them.

I set my course for Titusville to meet an old friend and pick up some information about a name I found on the map at the library. I had e-mailed him the name and had a pretty good idea where the results would lead me.

CHAPTER

35

I love Merritt Island, but there is a section I don't frequent for personal reasons. I don't even take the time to drive through the area. It was bad enough I had to see the homes around Honeymoon Lake, so traveling farther south below the Pineda was not something I wished to do. At this time, however, it was something I needed to do.

In this area of prestigious gated homes there are houses with property running from river to river. Old Route 3, or South Tropical Trail, looks as if it needs permission to slide along the Indian River through the properties only the wealthy and privileged should be allowed to travel. I knew driving in this area would definitely draw attention to me from certain individuals, but if it didn't, I would make it my business to be noticed.

So off I went. After leaving my old friend's place of business in Titusville with my information in hand, I took U.S. 1 all the way down until I hit the Pineda Causeway. It was a stop-and-go tedious ride, but I wanted to take my time and give my friendly goons a chance to find and follow me, and they did.

Their tail was so obvious it wasn't funny. I was actually tempted to be a wise ass and stop to buy us all coffee and a few donuts, but that temptation slowly faded as I continued south.

We finally made it to the Pineda Causeway and traveled toward the beach and exited on South Tropical Trail. I cruised in the area I knew I would not be welcomed in. So I took my time, slowed to a crawl, and waited for what I was hoping would happen next.

I made a few passes in front of the location I was interested in when the flashing red lights of an unmarked cruiser pulled in behind me.

"License and registration, please," was the greeting I received from an unidentified voice.

"No problem, my good man," I answered.

After a few minutes the patrolmen didn't return, but the tall, skinny goon from my trailer arrived at my window, walking from his car that had slowly snuck up behind the cruiser.

"Mr. Anderson," he spoke quietly. "Would you be so kind as to accompany us down the road a bit? I have someone who would like to speak with you."

This saved me a lot of trouble. Getting into the location I intended suddenly had become much easier. "Certainly, show me the way, and I'll follow."

He returned a quick thank you and said, "I do believe you know where we're going?"

The patrolman pulled away and left as the dark sedan moved in front of me. I followed it to a gated home about one hundred feet away. The gates opened and we entered the long, palm-trimmed driveway leading to an enormous house that sat on the Banana River. The grounds were immaculate with sweeping views of the water. It also had a grove with oranges, pineapples, mangos, and every citrus tree you could imagine to one side of the estate. It looked much the way it must have been back in the days of plantations, Indians, and slaves.

"Please, wait here," shouted the muscle-bound goon who accompanied me into the foyer and was out of sight in seconds. I had no problem waiting, awed by the construction of this mini-palace with its vaulted ceilings, enormous columns, and long, reaching staircases that led to the upper level.

"If you would be so kind as to follow me," came a voice from my side as another goon showed up to escort me into the study.

The study was, without saying, exquisite. There were fireplaces on two walls and paintings of various individuals hanging in each corner of the room. A sitting area with leather-bound furniture large enough to sit a small army circled a large desk. At the desk sat a man; a very distinguished older man of about seventy, with slick gray hair, eyes of blue steel, and a face chiseled from granite.

"Tucker, have a seat," demanded the voice of authority.

From his tone and, of course, his power of suggestion, he was telling me what to do, not asking.

Therein lay my problem. Don't order me to do things.

I hesitated for a second and then placed myself opposite him as he sat with his hands folded on his desk. His goons stayed stationed in the room, both standing off to the side, at attention.

What assholes, I thought to myself, *you couldn't pay me enough to take orders from this asshole and stand there like a trained chimp.*

"Tucker, I want to personally give you the opportunity to explain to me why you are pursuing this case and not going with the official findings from the chief medical examiner like all other nice reporters are doing."

Wait a minute, don't answer that.

Yeah, I guess I will.

"Why not go with the official findings? Well, that's simple, because it's all bullshit, that's why, and you of all people know it," I simply replied, holding up a manila envelope I had picked up in Titusville.

It was not the answer he expected as he stared at the envelope. "Tucker, you are way out of your league here. You're nothing but a two-bit local sports reporter—and a lousy one at that."

I looked over and the tall skinny goon had a smirk on his face.

Asshole!

"I have been very patient with you this past week and hoped you'd take it upon yourself to back away. You're sticking your nose into a very complicated area right now. I am telling you, Tucker, to back away."

"Back away?" I said. "Judge, that's not in my nature."

Judge Arnold David Galley was one of the wealthiest and most powerful men in Central Florida. His family had been here for generations and had amassed enormous amounts of property and influence, mostly through questionable means. Coercion, bribery, threats, and even murder were all ways in which this family operated early on when they were the first white settlers in the area. I knew the family was corrupt, but never put two and two together until that first day at the library when I looked at the old map from the 1800s and noticed a familiar name.

I gave the name I saw on the map to an old private detective friend up in Titusville to run a check on it. With the click of the mouse, he was able to trace the family tree of the judge to the captain. The name had changed over the years to cover up the captain's deeds and to separate the judge and his other family members from an embarrassing past. To be honest, the family continued to be a group of assholes and the name change really didn't help their reputation.

* * *

Captain Wilson Gale, Crystal Saunders' husband, was Judge Galley's great-great-grandfather. Before the Civil War, the good captain had purchased land through threats and coercion, then later combined all the plantations in the area into his own. It wasn't uncommon for him to use intimidation and murder as a means of communication. The murder of Osci and his family was only the tip of the iceberg for what Captain Gale was capable of and did. At the end of the Civil War he had also found himself dishonorably discharged from the cavalry after being implicated in the massacre of a tribe of Indians in the Ocala region. Later he was charged and acquitted in the murder of a neighboring plantation owner.

But the straw that broke the proverbial camel's back happened when the captain's second wife was found dead of a gunshot wound to the back. That one was impossible for him to get out of. The wife's family was very influential and a lengthy trial threatened to ensue.

Captain Gale's family, knowing they needed to do something to save themselves from ruin, sold out their own patriarch. After a few bribes, the captain was deemed mentally incapable to stand trial and committed to an insane asylum up in Georgia. It was rumored he had contracted syphilis and his mind deteriorated. The family then decided the best course of action was to change their last name, at least its spelling, and continue as usual with their illegal business. The family even compiled wealth by being the first bootleggers in the area during Prohibition. Let me restate that. They were the *only* bootleggers, having murdered anyone who dared get in their way.

Judge Galley had continued the family tradition. With bribes and payoffs he bought elections, amassed wealth and property. He became one of the biggest crooks the central part of the state had ever seen. The problem—everyone was scared of him.

* * *

I did know the family name meant everything to the judge, even more than money. He was willing to do anything to protect it, especially in an election year.

The judge shook his head. "You leave me no other choice, Tucker, but to—"

"To what?" I interrupted. "You going to try to blow me up again like you did last night?"

A gasp came from a shadow that had just entered the corner of the room. "Arnold!" she screamed. "You promised me you wouldn't hurt him!"

I turned around. A very stunning woman, aged by time and drink but still attractive, stepped into view.

The judge roared, "Edna, I told you to stay out of this! Go back to your room and have another drink."

The woman whirled around and looked at me. "Tucker, please leave this alone and let things be, please?"

I had a hard time looking at her, but managed to say, "Fuck off, and mind your own business."

The judge quickly stood. "Tucker, don't you dare speak to your mother that way."

CHAPTER

36

"My mother?" I shouted. "I have no fucking mother! To me she died years ago!"

"Tucker, please don't speak that way," she cried.

"Screw you, you whore. You left Dad and me for this…this…this piece of shit."

Tension quickly escalated to a crescendo pitch. The goons stepped toward me as the judge's face grew hotter. For a minute no one said a word.

* * *

I was furious. My mother had come home one day and abruptly announced she was leaving Dad for a better life. She promised a small boy of four she would always be with him and take him to her new home every weekend. Soon weekends, holidays, and eventually years passed by and my mother slowly faded away to a sad memory. She had decided that a new life of money and prestige was worth more than my dad or me. Through the tears of a little boy and the broken heart of a father, we had managed to survive.

* * *

Breaking the tense silence, the judge barked out, "Edna, I told you from the beginning he and his father were nothing but white trash."

I took a quick step toward the judge, but was cut off by the tall, skinny goon. "I wouldn't do that," he said with a smirk on his face.

Don't hit him, don't hit him, don't hit him, I repeated to myself.

Fuck that!

I pivoted on my left leg and caught him flush on the jaw with a right hook. He went stumbling backward and landed on top of a glass-topped coffee table, shattering it. The other goon reached for his gun.

"Don't!" yelled the judge, holding up his hand.

I picked up the envelope I had carried in and tossed it on the desk. "Here you go, big man," I said sarcastically. "Enjoy your reading."

"Tucker, you won't get away with this. No one will ever see your copy of this!" he shouted.

"Judge, you think I'm that dumb? Even a white piece of trash like me knows to make a lot of copies. They're on their way to every major news organization from Miami to Atlanta, and one is in safe keeping with some side notes in case I happen to mysteriously disappear. Remember, it's an election year, any candidate news is big news."

I headed to the door as the goons who were picking up their buddy quickly returned their attention to me.

"Let him go," the judge mumbled, his teeth clenched in fury. "I'll take care of this myself, and you stop your crying and get out of here!" he directed toward his wife.

I walked to the door and was actually feeling good about myself. Seeing my mother—or should I say that woman—after all these years was okay. I had always thought I would have trouble with it, but it wasn't so bad. There is always room for forgiveness, but when my dad died and no call came from her, I wrote her off as being dead and resigned myself to burying her memories with him.

I reached the door and told an approaching butler I could let myself out. I took a breath of fresh air and headed off to complete my mission.

CHAPTER

37

Darkness settled over the area as my boat glided out onto the river. A late season storm had started to develop on the eastern horizon. The sky darkened and the wind ruffled the waves as a late November breeze picked up. A clap of thunder shook overhead and lightning stroked the tree line and electrified the air.

I had the feeling I was being driven on a course I felt compelled to follow. I swung south along Merritt Island's western shoreline and throttled the Whaler to a steady crawl as I looked for a creek that had come to me more than once in my dreams. The sky continued to flash and my vision became blurred as a light mist settled along the edge of the shoreline.

Where was I to turn? What had been so clear in my dreams now became confusion. The bundle at my feet had to be delivered to its rightful resting place—I had believed this from day one, and I needed to follow this strange feeling and attachment I had.

As I slowed and stared into the mist the hair on my neck stood up. To the left of me, a figure loomed.

Standing in his canoe, Osci waved for me to follow him. The creek I could not find seemed to appear out of nowhere. Reeds had grown over the entrance of the small canal and I was able to use it to enter another body of water—Honeymoon Lake. Damn, I was shocked by this location. Was it a coincidence?

The storm continued to intensify as lightning shook all around me, yet the feeling of being isolated from the elements prevailed.

Another opening among the reeds appeared as I reached the southern shoreline, and Osci again waved at me, a gesture to continue and follow him. I traveled for at least half a mile into the marsh, the sides of the small creek seeming to open up for me as it twisted along.

The back woods area was not one I was familiar with, and I lost sight of the Indian. As I turned the corner I spotted his canoe beached on a shallow sandbank.

I quickly beached my Whaler, but was uncertain what to do next. The storm finally started to subside, and the trail illuminated in front of me.

As I looked, the lightning highlighted the path to its end, about fifty feet away, where Osci stood. Once he caught my attention, he motioned me to come.

I hesitated. Walking though the swamp wasn't a great idea at night—or at any time, for that matter. Every possible horrible scenario crossed my mind. I continued anyway, but seeing Osci gave me a sense of reassurance. I picked up the package and stepped onto the sand.

After a step, I froze! To my left sat a large gator, the one I saw in my dreams with Osci. It didn't move but seemed to look at me with a gleam in its eye. I couldn't move, but Osci smiled and continued to wave with his "follow me" gesture, and so I did.

I walked a short distance through the mangroves and cypress trees and went to him holding the bundle I knew belonged to him. But Osci had disappeared! I was left standing alone in a small clearing next to a huge cypress tree.

As I stood there I seemed to be drawn to a nearby spot, the same spot I had seen in my dreams. But where did Osci go?

I walked to the cypress on my right and stopped, suddenly noticing Osci standing there with his head bowed. I looked—and what I saw brought me to my knees. For there, still in chains, fastened to the tree, were the skeletal remains of Osci and his beloved Crystal.

They had been abandoned, left for the elements to destroy, almost one hundred and forty years ago. Their remains still were tightly held by the chains.

I needed no more instructions; I laid the bundle at the base of the tree and slowly removed the bones.

Lightning again electrified the air and a light rain began to fall. The healing process began. With my bare hands I began to dig at the base of the cypress tree to construct a shallow grave. There I buried Osci, Crystal, and their son.

In ceremony, I placed two lighted candles on each end of the grave and slowly waved another through the air in a circular motion above each. The thunder cracked and I was done. I covered the grave, rose to my feet, and with the difficulty of a heavy heart, I started back to the boat.

I looked back one last time and was not surprised to see the spirit of Osci standing with Crystal holding their son to his heart. He nodded in appreciation as I smiled, never looking back again, and left.

As I stepped toward the canoe I remembered the gator was not far from where I had landed. As I approached, I saw he was still there and watching my every move. He raised his head, turned toward me, and for the life of me I swear he smiled as he lowered himself into the water and disappeared.

I maneuvered my little Whaler back down the creek and onto Honeymoon Lake heading back toward the Indian River. The sky was now clear; any remains of the storm had disappeared. The sky looked as bright and full of stars as I had ever seen it, and I do believe they where twinkling at me.

CHAPTER

38

Brevard Daily
Beachside Skeleton Not a Ventara Victim

Tucker Lee Anderson, Staff Reporter

Recent forensic results have all but confirmed the beach-side skeletal remains are not those of Eddie Ventara's last victim, as many news agencies have reported.

Ventara, the Central Florida child murderer who was sitting on death row awaiting his execution for the murder of his other victims, was recently found dead in his cell of an apparent suicide at Raiford State Prison.

Karla Santiago, the medical examiner originally assigned to the beachside case, has confirmed to this reporter that the forensic results originally processed in fact state the remains actually date back to the mid-1800s.

It leaves this reporter to question why then was an official statement released from the chief medical examiner and the county, stating that these were the final remains of Eddie Ventara's last victim?

Calls to the chief medical examiners and the Brevard County Press Officer have not been returned.

The *Brevard Daily* will continue its investigation into this controversial cover-up with a three-part series. Beginning this weekend, the series will examine the past history of Brevard County and its settlers. It is with great hope that through examining our past ancestors, communities, politics, and economics, we will better understand why Brevard has become the pristine area it is today.

When the newspaper first hit the stands, all hell broke loose. Not in a bad way, but actually in a good one. A lot of people started to play the "cover your butt" game as people started to question the hierarchy of the county and their elected officials.

The following days for the *Brevard Daily* were hectic, to say the least. Every news agency from New York to Miami caught wind of the story with its speculations and ascended on us like flies on...well, you know, like flies on shit. They all wanted their personal interviews and a piece of the story.

Mitch couldn't be any happier. The newspaper's circulation had all but tripled and the larger papers wanted his permission to reprint the investigative reporting by yours truly in their papers. Mitch wheeled and dealed, and whenever we saw each other, he smiled and gave me the thumbs up. I even thought he blew me a kiss one time. He was happier than a pig in...well, you know.

I really owed Karla everything; she truly is a beautiful person. She had gone out on a limb for me, letting me run the story with her name attached. She being an accredited source sealed it. She figured she was better protected by getting things out in the open rather than keeping them hidden. What were they going to do now? Discipline or fire her for telling the truth? It was way too public for them to take action. She had them, and they knew it.

Craig was also on cloud nine. No one dared to mess with him at work. He was actually given a promotion to a higher class of detective, which meant more money, just to keep him happy and preoccupied so he didn't investigate what was really going on any further. He also had a new woman in his life, a gorgeous little second-grade teacher who had just moved down from up north.

As for me, I got to be a star for a while once again. But this time I didn't have to do it by shooting three-point shots. All I had to do was write what I experienced and knew to be true.

Requests to have me on a number of national morning television shows kept coming in, but I thought I'd play it cool and lay low, out of the spotlight, at least for now. I did, however, start my three-part series on the history of Brevard and early plantation life.

Now why would I choose that topic to start the series with? Funny, don't you think? Ah, I crack myself up sometimes.

Anyway, in my reports I was able to trace the activity of one prominent Brevard family and the illegal acts they had committed before a name change was issued. The changes were supposedly done to protect the other family members who could be harmed by such awful events perpetrated by a certain family member. The dilemma turned out to be that the entire family was actually pretty bad and corrupt, and it carried over from one generation to another. Guess it was in their genetic makeup. A few months after my story was printed, Judge Arnold Galley withdrew his name from the upcoming elections and quietly retired to his estate. This I did find a little unusual for the judge. I never figured he would slowly drift out of sight. It made me wonder why, and what he really could be up to.

I had all the proof of this in legal documents, so trying to go after me for libel just wouldn't work on his part.

I purposely didn't connect Osci, Crystal, and the baby to all this in my story, though I did mention it in a later article. They had been through enough. The embarrassment I'd cost the judge and his family was sufficient and exactly what I believe Osci would have wished for. It must have been, because I haven't dreamt of him lately, so I'll assume he's satisfied.

Personally, I was feeling great; the only thing I could think of to make this better was a nice little vacation. I hadn't had a real one in years, and Mitch was more than obliged to pay for it.

So off I went. Not to Disney, but to the adult amusement park we call Key West.

EPILOGUE

Key West is one of those magical places. Balmy breezes, sunshine, and the greatest assortment of people you could ever find in any one place. The town itself is just a version of an adult amusement park. Everything and anything can be found here. If you stay long enough, you'll never be surprised or disappointed.

It is also a great place to just hang out and relax. Laze the day away sitting by the turquoise Atlantic Ocean or Gulf of Mexico, spend the afternoon deep sea fishing or just sitting at a bar on Duval Street and people watch. I personally prefer the latter.

A vacation is what I needed and, to be honest, deserved. So when I thought of a quick getaway, Key West was the place. Jimmy Buffett said in one of his songs, "I took a weekend off to recall the whole year." Well, that's exactly what I was doing. My reflection was really over the past couple of weeks, not a year, but the phrase fit, so why not use it?

Sitting by the pool with a drink in my hand and the sun on my face made it easier to reflect, especially since it was about the most important part of my life—my family.

Carl and Jessie were great, and Daddy being a bit of a local celebrity made dealing with Daddy a little more enjoyable—at least for the time being. Sure, there were the usual comments, but Daddy being talked about in a positive way made things more enjoyable.

The ex actually stopped being a complete ass to me. She still had her moments of being a bitch, but her friends now talked me up in a positive way. I know that pissed her off, but what was she to say? Yeah, we still didn't care too much for each other, but at least there was an element of civility whenever we had to talk.

I still missed Nan terribly. I guess it's a good thing, and having family matters set in their rightful place was a positive. Knowing Nan could always pop in on me at any time gave me a feeling of comfort. I'm also pretty sure if I screw up something, she'll be back to voice her opinion.

I took a sip of my margarita and shifted in the lounge chair to get the greatest amount of sun. It was late afternoon, so planning the evening's events was my next concern.

"Would you like another drink?" she asked as she rose gracefully out of the pool.

I smiled and said, "Nah, thanks anyway, I want to save room for a few more later on."

"Well, it's getting late, and if you want to get over to Mallory Square for the sunset celebration, we better get cleaned up." She smiled at me and started to walk back toward our room.

"I'll shower first, if you like," she said with another smile over her shoulder as she shook the water out of her hair and let the breeze catch it. "But don't forget the shower is big enough for the two of us."

I smiled and watched as she pouted her lips at me and swayed her hips back and forth as she walked away, just to tease me.

Boy, I love being teased!

Hmm, room for two, I thought to myself, *that's not a bad idea.* I quickly jumped up to chase her in. Before I did, I noticed the light blinking on my cell phone; I had received two new texts.

One was from Craig saying, "Hey, buddy, hope you're having a great time in the Keys with your friend. Don't do anything I wouldn't do or have done." He had added a smiley face to the end.

Wise ass, I thought to myself. *No wonder we get along so well. He really is my best friend.*

The other text was from Mitch. "Hey, superstar, give me a call as soon as you can, I got a good one for ya."

I'd answer them both later on. Without wasting any more time, I grabbed my towel and ran in after Karla, hoping to help soap her up.

Ahhh, life is good.

ACKNOWLEDGMENTS

Many thanks go out to everyone who encouraged me with the creation of *Beneath The Dune*. To my family and especially Michele, you have been the backbone and my foundation along the way.

To Cyndi, Carol, and Toni, for being the first to read and review my novel. To everyone at the Writer's Workshop, especially John, Len, Holly, and Melanie, as well as all the others for their continuous support and positive feedback.

Walter Ramsay

Look for Walter's next book,
Coastal Access coming soon

For more information visit:
www.walterramsay.com
www.penabeachpress.comv

An excerpt from the forthcoming

COASTAL ACCESS

By Walter Ramsay

Certain days occur only once in a great while. The ones you enjoy, cherish, and place in your memory. Mornings are glorious with clear blue skies and a sun's warmth that tickles your senses. For Andy Babcock, or Drew, as his few friends called him, that's the way it was as he headed out to explore the area of Florida time forgot.

A low mist hovered over the marshland and lake region that made up the western portion of Brevard County. The sun would gradually burn off the mist and a spectacular spring day would arrive.

Drew was the last of his kind—a loner who loved the isolation the land provided. As a purebred Floridian, Drew grew up in Cocoa where his family had resided for as long as he could remember. But the continuous growth of the area and influx of northerners for the space race gradually pushed him west of Interstate 95. It was the perfect place for someone who wanted to be left alone.

With no family to speak of, Drew lived alone, hunted for his food, and gathered all the necessities he needed from the natural resources of the area. The only contact he had with the outside world came when he intermittently visited the local corner store for a few staple items and an occasional beer. He shunned every creature comfort—no telephones, televisions, computers, cell phones, or World Wide Web; life was nice and simple. Everything he felt he needed could be found in his bungalow on a dirt road off of Route 532. People seldom if ever traveled the road or visited the area; its only existence was on the county tax map.

Today was like every other day for Drew. He woke up early to travel deep into the underbrush. He would check his traps and gather herbs and berries and be home before the sun reached its zenith. Hopes were always high for catching a fox, duck, or deer. The occasional gator was his only concern. However, they seemed to watch Drew as much as he looked out for them. The possibility of being skinned and turned into a stylish pocketbook seemed to be on the gators' minds as they stayed clear of his path.

As Drew walked, an unusual feeling came over him. Something was a little different. But what was it? He stood and listened and could hear a faint rumbling. He checked the sky for thunderheads, but saw none. The other day on his walk he had spotted a few white trucks racing across a remote area. It had seemed strange since no traffic ever came off the main roads.

Drew continued his walk and focused his attention on the deer trail he was now following. He walked carefully, not disturbing the surrounding area or leaving any tracks. Yet that strange feeling and the rumbling sound persisted.

From the corner of his eye, Drew spotted the source of the sound as two quads rounded the bend and approached.

"Hey there, buddy," one of the riders called out as they rolled to a stop next to Drew. Drew tightened the grip on his rifle as he looked at the two men in hunting gear with rifles slung over their backs. He hesitantly nodded a greeting.

"We haven't seen many other hunters out here. Are you alone?" one asked with a smile.

Drew said nothing, just nodded his head again and wondered if they could possibly be poachers.

"We were hoping," the smaller guy said, "that you might be able to point us in the direction of some good hunting."

"You're not going to catch anything with those noisy contraptions you're sitting on," he answered in disgust.

"Oh no, we get the whole silent hunting thing, we were actually looking to set up camp, sit for a while, and wait to see what comes our way," the same one responded.

Drew thought for a minute as he watched the guy who wasn't talking staring expressionlessly off into the distance. Without further hesitation or emotion, Drew responded, "Well, you could head down to Crane's Creek, about two miles south of here. It's a great place to camp. Pull out a little food and all the pickings will come your way."

As Drew pointed toward the south, the smaller of the two turned his head in interest to look, but the other guy remained like a statue, staring straight ahead.

"You say good things down there? Guess we could give it a try," he said as he motioned to the guy next to him to get moving along. "Thank you kindly," he added.

Drew nodded in return and started down his trail as the two strangers adjusted themselves in their seats before firing up those loud beasts.

Birds scattered, deer stood at attention, a lone gator slid into the murky water from its embankment as two shots echoed across the vast expanse of wetlands.

The sound of the two quads slowly faded into the distance as Drew Babcock lay with two gun shots in the back of his head. *Why? I don't understand* was the last thought running through Drew's mind as his life slowly trickled away.